THE CIRCLE OF BLOOD

THE CIRCLE
OF BLOOD

a forensic mystery by
Alane Ferguson

VIKING

VIKING

Published by Penguin Group

Penguin Group (USA) Inc., 345 Hudson Street, New York, New York 10014, U.S.A.

Penguin Group (Canada), 90 Eglinton Avenue East, Suite 700, Toronto, Ontario, Canada M4P 2Y3
(a division of Pearson Penguin Canada Inc.)

Penguin Books Ltd, 80 Strand, London WC2R 0RL, England

Penguin Ireland, 25 St Stephen's Green, Dublin 2, Ireland (a division of Penguin Books Ltd)

Penguin Group (Australia), 250 Camberwell Road, Camberwell, Victoria 3124, Australia
(a division of Pearson Australia Group Pty Ltd)

Penguin Books India Pvt Ltd, 11 Community Centre, Panchsheel Park, New Delhi – 110 017, India

Penguin Group (NZ), 67 Apollo Drive, Rosedale, North Shore 0632, New Zealand
(a division of Pearson New Zealand Ltd.)

Penguin Books (South Africa) (Pty) Ltd, 24 Sturdee Avenue, Rosebank, Johannesburg 2196, South Africa

Penguin Books Ltd, Registered Offices: 80 Strand, London WC2R 0RL, England

First published in 2008 by Viking, a member of Penguin Group (USA) Inc.

10 9 8 7 6 5 4 3 2 1

LIBRARY OF CONGRESS CATALOGING-IN-PUBLICATION DATA

Ferguson, Alane.

The circle of blood : a forensic mystery / by Alane Ferguson.

p. cm.

Summary: As she uses her knowledge of forensic medicine to investigate the death of a young
runaway, seventeen-year-old Cameryn Mahoney, an assistant to her coroner father, worries that
her secretive mother may be involved.

ISBN 978-0-670-06056-6 (hardcover)

[1. Coroners—Fiction. 2. Forensic sciences—Fiction. 3. Mothers and daughters—Fiction.
4. Mystery and detective stories.] I. Title.

PZ7.F3547Cj 2007

[Fic]—dc22

2007010420

Printed in the U.S.A.   Set in Bookman ITC light   Book design by Jim Hoover

To my sister,
Dr. Serena Nolan,
who heals lives with
loving care and fills
hearts with music

THE CIRCLE

OF BLOOD

Chapter One

CAMERYN MAHONEY WAS surprised to see the blood on her hand.

She'd always been careful to tug on a pair of latex gloves, the whisper-thin barrier she wore every time she processed a body. Today's accident had been worse than anything she'd experienced thus far as assistant to the coroner. The decedent had been a young man—one Benjamin Baker, organ donor. Sixteen and dead, with Christmas only weeks away. In a bizarre twist, the car's crumpled radio had played on, some country version of "Jingle Bells." She'd listened to it as she picked through the wreckage, trying not to step in the blood that seeped from his gaping neck into an ever-widening arc across the snow.

Now, sitting in her driveway outside her own home, her

car in neutral, Cameryn stared at the red mark on her hand. There must have been a tiny tear in her glove that had allowed the fluid to seep in. With the lightest touch of her fingertip, she traced the silver dollar–sized stain, a scarlet web whose threads disappeared into her finger line. Her own coroner stigmata.

"Cammie—come into the kitchen. You're going to catch your death from the cold! Do you hear me, girl? Come inside where it's warm."

Startled, Cameryn looked up to see her Irish grandmother standing less than ten feet away on their back porch, the door held ajar by her hip. Stout and white-haired, she scooped the air with a thick arm. Her mammaw's lips were pressed into a frown, and her pale eyes, set deep into her face, were lit with worry.

Cameryn rolled down the window. "In a minute, Mammaw," she said. "I just need a little time to myself right now. I'm . . . thinking."

"But it's almost noon," her grandmother protested. "Since the crack of dawn you've been out looking at Lord-knows-what. Gruesome, horrible things. A dead body before the day's even begun. It's wrong, is what it is."

"Mammaw, it was just a car accident."

Where some older women had skin that wrinkled like parchment, her mammaw's thick skin sagged into deep grooves, especially on the sides of her mouth, suggesting a perpetual frown. "Come inside. Have some lunch.

Or breakfast, if you'd prefer. I'll make you whatever you want. Food heals the soul."

"Thanks, Mammaw. It's just, right now, I want to be alone. I'll be there soon, though, okay? I promise."

Her grandmother shook her head and closed the door so that the plastic Christmas wreath swayed against the glass until it lost momentum and stopped. Pressing a button, Cameryn put the window up, and she returned to her own personal cocoon. She sat, staring, her mind drifting once again to the mangled wreckage she'd discovered on the road.

Blood. There had been so very much blood. She pressed her fingertips into her closed eyes, but the images still played behind her lids.

The gaping hole of Benjamin's neck, the bulb of his vertebrae gleaming white, the feathers of steam from where the still-warm liquid met cold asphalt, the geometry book peppered with blood. Centrifugal force had caused Benjamin's decapitation. Patrick Mahoney, Cameryn's father and Silverton's coroner, had explained this as they'd studied the remains. The car's door had sheered off, and the body lay half in, half out of the mangled vehicle. Benjamin's fingers curled against the snow, as if he were playing a keyboard.

"This young man didn't wear his seat belt. A car protects the body in a crash, and without a restraint—

well, you see what can happen," her father told her.

Cameryn nodded. She'd already taken her first sweep of pictures. Propping the camera on her hip, she said, "At least it was quick."

"He never knew what hit him." Her father sighed as he surveyed the body, jotting notes in his red plastic binder. "We'd better get a sheet."

"I'll do it. I packed one in the car."

She turned to go but found she suddenly couldn't move. Patrick had drawn her into a tight embrace, so close she could smell the wood smoke embedded in his black regulation parka. The edge of the binder bit into her back.

She felt swallowed up, suffocated by her father's sheer physical size. A tall man with a barrel chest and heavy brows, he had both a build and coloring so different from her own. The once-red hair was still dense as grass, but age was turning it a snowy white. His ruddy complexion made his blue eyes seem glacial. She, on the other hand, had inherited her mother's dark curly hair, warm, golden skin, and brown eyes, as well as her mother's diminutive height.

"Dad," she said into his parka, "I can't breathe. And we need to start looking."

"Sorry." He released her with a rough kiss to the top of her head. "You're right, there's still a job to do. I need to find the rest of this guy." Squinting, he scanned the army of trees. "It is not going to be easy."

"I know."

The car had crashed on the Million Dollar Highway, a narrow, twisting two-lane road that folded back on itself like tossed-away ribbon. To the west, Colorado's San Juan Mountains loomed above them, while to the east, the ground cut away into a deep valley riddled with spruce. "The problem is," her father murmured, "that head could be anywhere. I've seen them sail a quarter mile or more, which means it could have gone down the mountainside. If it did, we're screwed."

"We can at least figure out the trajectory."

"How's that?"

She told him the amount of blood contained in a skull and how, once it became airborne, blood trailed from the base of the neck like paint until the head landed back on the ground. Find the blood and track it to the end, following the splatter like a trail of crumbs. Her father seemed impressed, asking if she'd learned that from her forensic books. Unlike her grandmother, he approved of her dream of becoming a medical examiner.

"That's good, Cammie, but reality is harder than theory. I'll do the search while you stay with the decedent until the sheriff arrives." He looked at his watch, tapping its face with his fingertip. "Something must have happened to hold up Jacobs. He should've been here by now."

It took a moment for her to process what her father

was saying. A chill crept through the soles of her cowboy boots and up past her faded jeans until it spread all the way into her chest. Once again, he was shutting her out. Before, they'd worked their cases as a team, but lately he'd been finding excuses to leave her at home. If she hadn't taken the call about this morning's crash, she suspected she would have been left behind on this one, too. "Wait," she protested. "I don't want to stay here with the body—I want to go with you."

"And I want you to stay here. Do the inventory, okay?"

At that moment a semi appeared, blowing black smoke from an upright exhaust pipe. She heard a squeal as the driver engaged the brakes. The man, riding high in his cab, goggled the wreckage. Her father's disgust deepened when the man honked his horn. "Keep moving!" Patrick yelled, his arm circling like the blades on a windmill. "Go on!" Black smoke belched from the truck's exhaust pipe as it strained to regain momentum up the steep hill. "People always want a bloody show. Cammie, get that sheet. This fellow shouldn't be gawked at. I'll be back as quick as I can."

"We'll go twice as fast with me searching."

"I'll take it from here," he said pleasantly.

Although lately he'd taken to wearing turtlenecks instead of his usual T-shirts, today he was dressed as he used to be: workmen's boots and his frayed coroner's cap with a star stitched in golden thread. But despite his familiar touches, there was something new in his demeanor.

He, who had often pried into his daughter's inner life, had himself become evasive. She could sense it.

"Do you think I've lost my forensic touch?" she asked.

"Hardly." Opening the binder, he clicked his pen, signaling they were done. "Everyone knows you're a prodigy." He peered at the form, muttering, "Cameryn Mahoney, Angel of Death. You've got quite a reputation around town." After scribbling a few lines, he held out the binder. "Okay, you're up."

But she refused to extend her hand. Crossing her arms, she hugged her sides. Her father's exasperation was etched in every line on his face. "Take it," he commanded.

"If you're going to shut me out, you can at least tell me why."

"For Pete's sake, you don't need to see a severed head." Jabbing the folder toward her, he said, "The face holds the soul, Cammie. Just—do the inventory."

"What's the real reason?"

Her father sighed. Slowly, the folder dropped to his side. Another truck crept by, its engine clattering like an old sewing machine, but this time they ignored the rubberneckers. "For one thing," he finally said, "I promised your grandmother."

This didn't surprise her. Her mammaw was convinced that cutting into the dead was the devil's business. Her father, though, had always been on her side. "Why did you make that promise?"

"Because the last case we worked on put you in danger. For now, at least, she wants you to stop." He grinned, trying to soften her up. "You know how she can be when her Irish dander's up. Just humor her, all right? Humor me."

Inside, Cameryn groaned. This again.

"But this *job*," she argued, "is the reason I'm being courted by a top forensic school. Besides, this case is not a homicide—it's a car wreck. Please, both of you, quit worrying about me. You said 'for one thing.' So, what's the other thing?"

He took a step closer, his eyes full of appeal. "You're struggling. There've been so many changes in your life that I want to keep anything that can hurt you as far away as I can. You can tell me anything, Cammie, and I'll help. No matter what it is. Or who."

At that moment, she became aware of a bird cawing overhead and the whisper of wind through the pines and the way her father's feet had planted in the snow like pylons. For some reason she registered these things—the mountain sounds and Patrick's stolid legs, the blinding whiteness of the snow, the coldness of the air in her lungs, mingled with the pungent smell of truck exhaust. It was then that she understood: this was not a conversation about some*thing*, this was about some*one*. Her father had been talking about Hannah, the mother Cameryn had never known, the woman who had unexpectedly been resurrected in their lives only weeks before.

"You're worried about Hannah," she answered. "That's what this is all about."

Patrick's silence told her all she needed to know.

"Dad, she's— I just want to spend time with her. You said you'd let me figure things out on my own, and that's what I'm doing. She's my mom."

"Genetically. A womb doesn't make a mother. And since we're opening this box, how long is Hannah going to stay in Silverton? Doesn't she have a life in New York? She was supposed to come and go, but she's still here."

"I—I don't know." It was the truth. Her mother had returned, but she was elusive, as vague about her plans as she was her thoughts. "Hannah told me she's just taking it a day at a time. She doesn't tell me a lot. She . . . paints."

"She paints." Patrick scoffed. "Hannah doesn't talk, she paints. Do you have any idea how crazy that sounds?"

"Don't say that!"

The words echoed against the granite mountainside. *That, that, that,* rang through the air and her father stared, as though if he tried hard enough, he might somehow burn Hannah from his daughter's mind. When she could no longer return his gaze, she watched the victim's math book as it lay there on the road, splattered with blood, its pages turning gently in the winter wind.

"Be careful," Patrick told her, his voice low. Placing a finger beneath her chin, he raised her face until she was forced to look into his eyes, which had become once again warm, fatherly. "I loved her once, too. But there are reasons you need to be cautious. Has she told you the story of how Jayne died?"

Shaking her head, she mouthed the word *no*. Of course she had asked. Countless times she'd tried to fathom details from the depths of her mysterious mother, but whenever she'd pressed, Hannah had turned away. In this delicate chase of daughter courting mother, Cameryn felt as though she'd lose if she pushed too hard.

"Before you give up your heart, find out what happened that day. I think it's important."

"Why can't you tell me?"

"A long time ago, Hannah promised to stay away and I promised to stay quiet. Secrets were put in place to protect you. But you tell her for me that if she breaks the deal, I will, too. You're slipping away from me, Cammie. She's giving me no choice."

"Dad." She stopped there, because the words she wanted to say were jammed in her throat. Eyes brimming with tears, she asked, "Why does it have to be this hard?"

"Oh, baby. Sweetheart, I'm sorry." Pulling a blowing strand of hair away from her face, he hooked it gently behind her ear. With the edge of his thumb he wiped a tear that rolled down the side of her cheek. "Cammie, it's just . . . when I saw that dead kid, I kept thinking about you and me and how time runs out. I— This is not the time or the place."

Before he could finish, lights flashed from the top of a white Durango, Silverton's four-wheel-drive police car. The blue and red dazzled like bottled rockets.

"Well," he sighed, "here they come." Patrick's brows knit together and he closed his eyes. When he opened them he'd become, once again, Silverton's coroner. "We've got a job to do. No matter what, we have to do it."

Blood had pooled against the side of Patrick's boot; his heel cleaved a print of red as he stepped toward the approaching car.

"Dad," she'd cried. "Wait!"

At that moment car doors slammed as Sheriff Jacobs, along with Deputy Justin Crowley, made his way toward the crumpled car.

"Sorry we're late. We had a snafu at the office," Jacobs declared as he approached the mangled car. He balled his hands on his hips as he surveyed the scene. "My God, Pat, what a mess."

"Oh, man, look at that," Justin said as he caught sight of the corpse. "Where's the head?"

"Haven't found it yet," Patrick replied. "I checked out the wallet—the kid's name is Benjamin Baker, resident of Durango. Cammie's done the first sweep of photos. She's going to stay back and do inventory while we search."

Sheriff Jacobs made a sound in the back of his throat. His features were sharp. His gray, thinning hair was hidden beneath a sheriff's hat that had actual earflaps. Small in stature, Jacobs was the kind of man whose motions were quick, impatient. Ever since Cameryn's father had hired her, the sheriff had radiated disapproval whenever Cameryn was on the scene. This time, though, he barely seemed to notice her. His already small eyes seemed to disappear as he squinted. "Guess we can skip calling the EMTs. Don't need an emergency team to check for a heartbeat if he don't got a head."

"That's what I thought," her father said. "I already declared time of death at five minutes before we received the first call. That makes it oh-six-hundred hours."

Sheriff Jacobs scribbled the number on his own notepad.

Rubbing his hands together, Justin blew on his fingers, his eyes surveying the scene until they rested on Cameryn's, lingering.

Are you okay? Justin mouthed. Cameryn nodded in reply. Justin's dark hair, too long for regulation, hung into his eyes; there was a slight shadow of stubble across his chin. Although he'd come from New York only five months earlier, Justin had already embraced Silverton's casual style. His brown leather bomber jacket had been broken in along with his jeans; the only thing that marked him as police was the badge he wore on a cord around his neck.

"Get out the cones, Deputy," said Jacobs.

Dutifully, Justin went to the back of the car and popped the trunk. A stack of orange cones appeared in his arms, which he then set up around the perimeter of the wreckage like dominoes.

Patrick said, "All right, then. Are you men ready for the hunt?"

Sheriff Jacobs gave a terse nod. "We don't want critters dragging that head away into the underbrush. If that happens, we might never find it. One thing, though, Pat, before we go." He and Patrick leaned close, murmuring something Cameryn could not hear. She stood, watching, unsure of her next move, unaware Justin had come to her side. "What's up?" he asked softly. "You seem pretty . . . intense."

"Nothing."

"I know that look, Cameryn. I had it myself when I was your age."

In spite of herself, she felt a smile tug at the corner of her mouth. "You aren't that much older than me. You're twenty-one and I'm almost eighteen. Do the math."

"Ah, but I remember the good old days of teen angst. Come on, you seem upset. And by the way, where have you been? It's like you vanished from Silverton. Although it seems impossible that anyone could disappear in a town of seven hundred."

She shrugged. "I've been spending a lot of time with my mom. Plus getting ready for college and schoolwork and my other job and—"

"You don't need to explain," he told her. "I just wanted

to make sure you're all right." His eyes had narrowed. "Are you?"

"Crowley!" the sheriff barked. "You coming or what?"

Justin looked over the top of Cameryn's head as the sun lit a tiny scar, like a silver thread, on his chin. "On my way, sir." Then, to Cameryn, "I've got to go."

She gave his retreating figure a halfhearted wave as the three men disappeared into the woods. Alone with the wreckage, she tried not to listen to the garbled holiday tunes that thrummed from the radio. As quickly as she could, she turned it off, gingerly reaching past Benjamin's blood-soaked chest.

But she wasn't able to concentrate. Her motions, done by rote, couldn't silence the words that played through her in an endless loop. *Hannah promised to stay away and I promised to stay quiet.* What had her father meant? The question spun through her mind as she photographed, bagged, sealed, and signed, collecting bits of life, bits of death. Another car, this one with a woman behind the wheel, slowed on the Million Dollar Highway. Cameryn, in a perfect reflection of her father, waved the woman on with her own gloved hand, glad she'd already draped Benjamin's body, propping the cloth as much as she could to keep the blood from seeping through.

She was just finishing up when she heard her father's cry, less than a hundred yards away.

"I got it. Good Lord, I almost stepped on the thing. John, Justin, over here!"

Sheriff Jacobs darted through the trees with Justin close behind, the branches snapping underfoot. Straining to see, Cameryn stood on her toes, but the limbs were too thick. She heard the sheriff say, "You got the bag, Deputy?"

"Yeah, I got it."

Her father replied, "Let's do this right."

Cautious, she crept between the pines, careful to keep her body low. No one looked her way. She watched as her father gently lifted Benjamin's severed head by the ears to place it inside a garbage bag Sheriff Jacobs held taut between his hands. Benjamin's skin was milk-white and the mouth gaped, and even from her distance she could make out the eyes, wide and scared. A ring of snow, soaked with blood and tissue, encircled the base of his neck like a red chain.

"Careful, Pat," the sheriff warned. "We don't want to lose anything."

"Don't worry, I got it," he replied. "The trick is to ease it in."

After tying the plastic yellow handles into a bow, Patrick placed the head in a green athletic bag and zipped it shut. For a moment no one said a word. Then, as if by silent agreement, the three men kicked at the bloody snow with their boots until the red lay buried beneath a mound of white.

Unseen, she slipped back to her post and her clipboard, dutifully inventorying the rest of Benjamin's items until her father returned to announce that she should go home—he had to take the body to Durango and make a call to the victim's family, and he wanted to do it alone. She didn't argue.

Glad she'd driven her own Jeep to the scene, she'd climbed in and left. In her rearview mirror she'd watched her father, Justin, and the sheriff as they strapped the remains to the gurney.

Now, sitting in the driveway of her own home, Cameryn once again touched the smudge on her palm. Threads led from the center all the way to the edge of her hand, the blood like tiny filaments connecting her to the dead. She saw a truth in that stain. If the face indeed revealed the soul, then Benjamin's spirit had not been ready to leave its body. In that last split second—had she imagined it?—his face had contorted in shock at his own demise. Whatever he had left undone on earth would stay undone, with no do-overs, no reprieves. Unanswered questions would stay that way forever.

She looked at her green-shingled house, lit from within. Her mammaw was inside, waiting, but it took only a moment for Cameryn to decide. She put her car into reverse and pulled out into her street, her tires slipping in snow as she shifted into drive.

It was time to see her mother.

Chapter Two

"JUST *ASK* HER," Lyric instructed. "Tell her you want to know about Jayne. See what she says."

Cameryn pressed her new BlackBerry to her ear. "You're kidding, right? You want me to tell Hannah she's got to come clean or the 'deal' is off?"

"No," Lyric replied patiently. "Of course you'll have to soften it. The weird part is that I was ready to hang your mom out to dry before I met her, but I have to admit, Hannah's actually pretty amazing. She's a true artist with a lot of soul."

Cameryn smiled. Lyric, loud and large, was an artist herself. Given her penchant for all things mystic and a personality bigger than Silverton itself, a stranger would never have paired the science-loving Cameryn with the new-age Lyric. While Cameryn favored jeans and basic blue, Lyric's clothes had been recycled from the sixties. Psychedelic patterns, fringed jackets, and plastic jewelry the size of dinnerware were Lyric's staples. She changed her hair color as often as her shoes. Yet the roots of their friendship ran deep, stretching all the way back to fifth grade. Laughter was the cord that bound them.

"A word of advice," Lyric said. "You have to remember that your dad's opinion of Hannah is biased. I love him to death, but this is a competition. You're the prize."

"Some prize. I'm so messed up I can't think straight."

"Science-heads such as yourself are sort of messed up by definition."

"Excuse me, science-heads deal in facts. This woo-woo-touchy-feely stuff is your domain, which is exactly why I needed you to tell me how to do this thing with Hannah. How do you *make* someone talk?"

"You say, 'I know this is hard, but understanding what happened in my past is important to me.' And did you just call me 'woo-woo'?"

"Your hair is purple. I think you qualify." From the front seat of her Jeep Cameryn scanned the upper floor of the Wingate, the bed-and-breakfast where her mother had set up house. Leaning forward, she peered over the steering wheel so that she could see the top of the home. Beneath a gable she saw her mother's window, lit from within. With a start, Cameryn realized Hannah's outline was clearly visible, a dark space against the light.

"She's watching me, right now!" Cameryn cried. "Hannah knows I'm here."

"Good! Honestly, if you can deal with a headless corpse, you can handle your own mother. Just *talk* to her! It's not that hard."

Peering anxiously, Cameryn chewed the edge of her cuticle.

"What can I do, Cammie?" Lyric asked. "You want me to light a candle? That's supposed to help, isn't it? It's a Catholic thing, right?" Cameryn could hear something rattle in the background. "I've got a whole box of birthday candles in my hand. I'll light the bunch if it'll help. Whatever works."

With a weak smile, Cameryn said, "No, just send me your good karma."

"That you've got. Now get in there. I'm babysitting and the rug rats are restless."

With that, Cameryn ended the call and dropped her BlackBerry into the pocket of her jacket. Stepping out of her Jeep, she looked up at the bright blue building.

The Wingate House had been painted the color of a clear blue Silverton sky. Built in 1886 by a Russian spiritualist named Emma Harris, the home was rumored to be haunted, although Cameryn had never accepted those wild stories. But now, as she looked at the moon-white face pressed into the glass, she half-believed. This ghost, though, was her own mother. Hannah was a different kind of spirit, but she haunted, just the same. Cameryn could read her mother's lips through the glass: "Come in," Hannah was saying. Then, like an apparition, she disappeared.

Cameryn entered the Wingate parlor, careful to shut the heavy door behind her. The owner had put Hannah into a room named the Adam and Eve Room, located on the second floor. Up the steep staircase Cameryn climbed, past a wall of old portraits. The door to her mother's room had been left open, and she stepped inside. An easel was set up at a right angle to the window, to capture the best light. And there, perched on a metal stool, sat Hannah, holding a paintbrush to her mouth. She wore jeans and a long-sleeved T-shirt speckled with colorful paint like bits of confetti. Although she seemed intent on her painting, she said, "Hello, Cammie."

"Hi, Hannah," Cameryn answered.

"'Mom,'" Hannah corrected. She smiled, flashing teeth. "I missed you today. I was up all night painting, and I kept thinking how much better it would have been if you'd been here to keep me company. There's something about this place that gives me energy. I feel like I can do anything!"

It still startled Cameryn to see her mother. In the mirror of Hannah's features she didn't see her own face, exactly, but an older version of herself, a Dorian Gray portrait in reverse. They shared the same high cheekbones and the identical large, dark eyes, the color of earth itself. Both of them were petite. Her mother, now forty-two, had kept her slender figure, her wiry frame. Gently curling hair that had only the beginnings of gray hung past her shoulders.

"Whether you realize it or not," Hannah said, "you've become my muse. Before I came to Silverton, I thought I couldn't paint anymore. Now I'm alive again. So, what have you been doing today?"

"Me? I had to work."

"At the Grand?"

"No," she answered carefully. "There was an accident. A boy died this morning."

"Oh." Her mother frowned. "That means you were working with your father."

"Yes."

Sighing, Hannah said, "Unfortunately, Patrick was always drawn to death. I never liked it. Truth be told, forensics is not my first choice for you as a career. I know it's your passion, but there's a whole world out there, beyond the grim. A doctor, maybe?"

"You sound like Mammaw."

"I do? Well, I'm sure that will be the first and the last time that happens. Your grandmother and I never saw eye-to-eye. She always hated me."

Cameryn's skin tingled with little pinpricks of gooseflesh. Tentatively she asked, "Why?"

But her mother, as always, ignored the question. "Let's talk about something more pleasant, like the fact that we're together. I'm so happy now." She returned to her painting. It was of an iris, with individual petals as big as her hand. Cameryn watched, unsure of her next move. She remembered that as a child she'd invented a fantasy mother, an angel-mom who'd scooped Cameryn into her arms to rain kisses on her head. The imaginary mother was so different from the flesh-and-blood woman now before her. Because she wanted it so much, Cameryn had been willing to play pretend, had become a partner in this false, manufactured intimacy. "I've always loved you," Hannah had said that first night.

I've always loved you, too. Cameryn had been hungry for it. But the closeness, she realized now, wasn't genuine. How could you really love what you didn't know?

Hannah dabbed paint on the edges of petals. The corners of her mouth lifted, ripples forming at the edges like a series of commas. "Cammie, sit down," she said. "You're just standing there. You're making me nervous."

A blue wing chair stood close to the easel, and Cameryn dropped into velvety cushions. The entire room had an overstuffed, plumped feel to it. The comforter was enveloped in eyelets, pillows had been tossed about, silk flowers bloomed from pots placed in every corner while curtains ballooned from the windows.

"Something has happened. I can sense it. Was it seeing the dead boy?"

"No. Well, yes, in a way," Cameryn said, wary of how to

begin. "I was bagging the vic's—I mean, victim's—property when I started thinking about how you never know when your time's up. The kid was just driving along, listening to the radio, and then *bam!*—he was dead."

"Is that what's worrying you?" Hannah asked, amused. "You think I'm going to die? Is that why you're so nervous?"

"No, that's not it." Cameryn's legs began to jiggle. She put her hands on her knees to stop them. "The thing is, you've been in Silverton two weeks and—"

"Three."

"Three weeks." She took a deep, wavering breath. "And I keep thinking that I still don't know about my life. Or yours. From before, I mean. With Jayne and all of that."

Her mother winced at the sound of the name. Cameryn could actually see Hannah's muscles tighten beneath her smock. "That past is over for me. I want you to get to know the person I am right now."

"But you can't separate the two."

"I've already told you how I feel. You need to respect my wishes."

"Right. But that's just the thing. *I* need to talk about it. I know it's hard. I've got this puzzle of my life with huge pieces missing." She felt a cold wave of disapproval emanating from her mother, so that right then Cameryn almost gave up. Had she not heard her father's voice in the back of her mind—*Secrets were put in place to protect you*—she might have turned back. *No,* she commanded herself. However impenetrable this ice wall seemed, she had to break through. "Just tell me the truth. What happened that day? When Jayne died. Is that why you left us?"

"Your father put you up to this." Hannah loaded her brush with paint, her fingers trembling as she swirled the tip into a deep purple, so dark it seemed almost black. "It's his way to get me out of town, to break us apart. He wants you to leave me."

It took a moment for Cameryn to process this, since it was backward from what she'd expected. Hannah to leave Cameryn, that was his obvious plan. But how could it be the other way around?

"Before you came to Silverton, you told me everything about my life was a lie."

"Not now, Cammie."

"But if you won't tell me what happened, then you're lying to me, too." Her words rushed into her throat so that she almost choked on them. "I thought I could trust you."

Her mother was silent.

Large slashes of purple, from deep plum to lavender, had been topped with a shining bright center, a gold-yellow, like a ray from the sun. These she covered with a brushstroke. Her movements were harder now as the bristles made a thwacking sound on the canvas.

"Hannah?"

"I'm not ready."

"This morning Dad and I had a . . . disagreement. It was about you. He told me secrets were put in place to protect me. He wouldn't tell me what he meant." Cameryn hesitated. Although she wasn't as good at reading people as Lyric, she sensed she was on sensitive ground. "Dad said that you've changed the rules, and that if you don't come clean, the deal is off." She waited a beat. "What is he talking about? What deal?"

The paintbrush stopped an inch from the canvas as Hannah held her arm unmoving, like a maestro waiting to begin. Then . . . nothing. Not a movement, not a sound. Cameryn's heart beat so loud she could hear it pulse in her ears, could feel her carotid artery flutter in her neck. Outside, someone laughed. She focused on that sound until it died away. "I didn't know I even *had* a sister until you sent me that painting and the letter. Dad and Mammaw lied to me."

"I never deceived you."

"But you're keeping secrets and that's the same. Father John says you can tell a lie without saying a word."

Her mother's hand hovered in the air as if it were a masthead pointing the way to another land. Why wouldn't Hannah speak again? Behind her, through the window, the mountain filled the frame all the way into the sky. Pure white snow had hidden everything, leaving the mountain featureless. It seemed as though, in the same way, her mother had been somehow erased. She'd gone away somewhere deep inside.

"Hannah?"

Her mother did not respond. In one last, desperate effort, Cameryn murmured, "I remember this dream I had, when I was little. It was about another girl. We were sitting in the gutter and I had a pretty pony named Cotton Candy and hers was blue and—somebody must have been hosing their driveway because there was a lot of water. And we were laughing, except then her pony floated away. Then the girl tried to take Cotton Candy, but I wouldn't let her."

The arm holding the brush drifted down into Hannah's lap, leaving a paint stain on the leg of her jeans. It spread like a bruise.

"Was that Jayne? Did that really happen?" Cameryn asked. And then, when her mother refused to answer, she demanded, "Say something!"

"I killed your sister."

The words hung in the air. *Killed. Your sister.* Cameryn couldn't take it in. "I'm sorry—what did you say?"

"I killed Jayne. I'm sure Patrick will be happy you know the truth at last."

Cameryn registered her mother's answer, but the wheels of her mind seized up.

"What . . . happened?" she finally whispered.

Her mother turned, her hair wrapped around her

neck like a scarf. Everything was dead except the eyes. She fixed them on Cameryn, her expression embalmed. In a flat, emotionless voice she said, "I backed out of the driveway. You two were always playing in the gutter, but that day I didn't see her. I felt the bump. I didn't stop. The tire left a tread mark on her dress—the yellow one with daisies. When I got out of the car, I saw her head in the water. Your father called me a murderer."

Cameryn didn't want to hear any more. Shutting her eyes, she commanded her mother to stop, screaming the word inside where Hannah couldn't hear.

"I've looked for girls ever since, trying to connect so I could remember. I'd see your faces everywhere—any girl with long hair, anyone who looked like they might need a mother. But even with all those strangers it was never the same. They can never be Jayne."

Cameryn had thought she'd prepared herself for every possibility—but not this. Never this.

Slowly, Hannah stood, peeling off the smock, releasing it to the floor in a crumpled heap. She went to the bed. Squatting, she searched under it for a pair of cowboy boots, which she tugged on over bare feet.

"What are you doing?" Cameryn asked, rising from the chair.

"I need to go out for a while."

"You're not a murderer, Hannah. I don't understand

why my dad said those things. It was an accident!"

"You want the truth? All of it?"

Cameryn nodded, even though she wasn't sure she did.

Hannah stood. "After the funeral, Patrick said I was an unfit mother. I killed your sister, so maybe I was. But I couldn't take it. So I tried to hurt myself. They . . ." She paused for only a beat. "I was put away. For a long time."

"Put away?"

"In a mental institution. I was there until they gave me some pills, and then I got better. Tegretol, which has been my savior. I'm all healed now. You probably don't believe it, but it's true."

Shocked, Cameryn said, "He—Dad never said a word."

"Not telling you was the only grace Patrick has ever given me. Well," she said, "now you know. You're free to hate me just the way Patrick wants you to." Wiping her hands on her jeans, Hannah walked to her dresser and picked up a set of keys. She plucked her jacket from a hook on the wall and shrugged it on. "I feel like I'm straining inside my own skin. Do you know what that's like? Just let me be for a while." Then, lifting her purse from a corner, she slung it over her shoulder and headed out the door.

Cameryn watched, frozen, unsure of her next move. Finally she stuttered out a protest, but Hannah was gone. Running, tripping, she made her way to the top of the stairs. "Wait! I understand! We need to talk about this. Mom! Please!"

But her mother didn't answer. Instead, the door to the Wingate slammed shut, rattling the stained glass in reply.

Chapter Three

IT WAS ONLY two o'clock in the afternoon, and dusk had already begun to descend on Silverton. Low-hanging clouds hovered at the bottom of the mountains and rolled into the streets, turning the air opaque. Cameryn could feel it, the clouds expectant, wishing they could burst open with snow.

Not wanting to return home, she'd parked her car in the back lot of the Grand Hotel. She needed to walk, to get her mind in order by moving her body. Her cowboy boots scuffed the shoveled wooden walkway as she made her way along Greene Street, weaving through the crowd of people who had come for Silverton's annual Christmas festival. Bright-eyed and red-cheeked from the cold, the milling crowd seemed happy, full up with Christmas spirit. Bowing her head so low the collar of her parka cupped her cheeks, she pressed on, trying not to envy their easy joy.

Suddenly a siren went off beside her, a single loud blast. Whirling around, she saw a police car. A window glided down and she looked inside to see Justin's smiling face. "Hey, Cammie, need a ride?"

"You about blasted out my eardrums," she said. She felt her face flush, as she realized the crowd's attention was now riveted on her. It was as if the entire street had stopped to stare, frowning at her with suspicion. "Everyone's looking at me," she hissed. "They think I'm under arrest or something."

"Hop inside and I'll read you your rights."

"You are *so* not funny."

"You want me to give this siren another blast?"

"All right, all right," she conceded, "just for a minute." She was only feigning reluctance. She'd missed him. Caught in the vortex of her new life, she hadn't connected with Justin in weeks, but in that there'd been a loss. It would be good to spend time with him again.

Cameryn opened the door and slid inside the Durango's gray interior. The air smelled like chicken noodles, which she realized came from the empty Cup-a-Soup he'd left on the passenger-side floor. "Sorry about that," he said, reaching down, and when he did so his hand brushed against her leg. He pulled it away quickly, apologetically, crumpling the cup before tossing it into the backseat.

"I'm on a budget, so this is my fine dining. I've got another cup if you'd like one. Did you eat lunch?"

"No," she answered, genuinely surprised to realize she hadn't. "I went to Hannah's right after the accident scene and then I decided to walk." Her hand went up, anticipating his next question. "And before you start asking, I don't want to talk about it. It's been a hard day and I'm . . . processing."

"Yeah, finding that head was surreal. When we put the gym bag on top of the guy's neck, it was . . . I don't know . . . grim. I've been thinking about that kid all day."

"Me, too," she said, relieved he thought she was processing because of Benjamin. The business of death didn't bother her the way it did others, a point that both fascinated and repelled her friends. The subject had come up just two days earlier as she lunched in the school's cafeteria. Crowded around Formica tables, stuffing their mouths with chicken fingers while they talked, the senior class had brimmed with college plans. Cameryn had just dipped a fry into her catsup when Crystal turned on her with almond-shaped eyes. "What about you, Cameryn? Are you still going to do all that death stuff?" When she'd nodded *yes*, the table had erupted. "How can you stand looking at such gross stuff?" was followed by "What about the maggots? Have you seen real maggots wriggling on a corpse?" after which came "I heard you already held a human liver and cut it up—that is so disgusting!" rounded out by a chorus of "How can you *do that*?" For as long as she could remember, her fascination with forensics had marked her as different. But for Cameryn, to peer inside a human body was a privilege. She understood that forensics was the last chance for the deceased to tell their stories; if she listened closely, they could whisper their secrets and she would translate.

"So, Justin, how come you're parked out here just watching the folks go by?"

Propping his wrists on the steering wheel, he said, "I guess sometimes there's a bit too much wassail downed at this festival. My job is to keep an eye out for drunks. This crowd looks pretty tame, though," he said, turning his palm up. "It's an interesting fair. Who knew so many folks'd come out for a snowmobile parade."

"There's also ice-sculpting and food and all kinds of stuff. Later on they'll have the dogsleds go by. It's really cool."

"Seriously? I thought they only had that kind of stuff in Alaska."

The second Saturday in December had been set aside for the festival. For as long as Cameryn could remember, she'd been out on the streets with the rest of them, sampling hot cider and watching winter games. This was the first time she'd ever forgotten.

"I'm liking all these people," said Justin. "Look at the rich folks there. . . ." He pointed to a couple, the man wearing an expensive-looking sheepskin coat, the woman swathed in fur. "I bet they're from Telluride. That dude's sunglasses cost more than my car. And check out all the snowboarders. I love those snowboard guys—their hats are *crazy*. I don't get what's up with the Gingham Girls, though. Are they in costume for something?"

"Who?"

"There, at the Bent Elbow. By that white truck."

Cameryn squinted. She saw a group of men, their skin lined from years in the sun, their hair cut into flat tops so short they appeared almost bald. Two women huddled to the side, whispering. Each had a long braid wrapped around her head in a gigantic loop, and one wore old-fashioned glasses with plastic frames from what Cameryn guessed was the seventies. Long dresses, sewn from red-and-blue gingham, hung to their ankles, peeking out from beneath long woolen coats. They wore mittens instead of gloves.

"Oh, those are polygamists from the Four Corners area. And they are women, not girls."

"You're kidding. Those arc *real* polygamists?" Justin's dark brows shot up in his forehead.

"Yeah. As in one guy with, like, seven wives."

"But those old men are geezers. How'd they get those girls—excuse me, women?"

"I don't think polygamy is about looks, Justin. I think

they're supposed to have all those wives so they can have a bunch of kids—it has something to do with their religion."

But Justin didn't seem to be listening to the part about children. Instead, he studied the women, who had moved apart, their eyes scanning the crowd. "Huh. Seven wives per guy." He grinned. "I like those odds. Where do I sign up?"

Cameryn hit his shoulder. "Sorry, here in Silverton we only have true Mormons—one man married to one woman—so unless you move away, you're out of luck. But we've got three Jehovah's Witnesses and an honest-to-God witch."

"A witch?" Justin looked impressed. "Who?"

"Look right there, at the woman standing next to that flower barrel. The one with the orange hair—that's Theresa Kennedy. She does the whole thing with casting spells and tarot cards and all of that. Next to her is Norland Match. *He's* the guy who was in Vietnam—he grows marijuana in his bathtub. Don't try to arrest him, though. Norland's got one of those medical permits."

It felt good to talk like this. People passed by in a leisurely but steady stream, and as she told the histories of Silverton's citizens, Cameryn felt her insides unkink. Although Silverton had become a tourist haven, eccentrics were still part of the town's fabric—from Leather Ed, who never bathed, to the madams and hookers buried in Hillside Cemetery. Watching the crowd, she thought about the fact that she was part of something bigger than herself, like . . . humanity. Her problems were just one part of an overall tapestry. She guessed each of these people had their own hidden stories from their pasts; even the strangers wearing candy-apple grins had secrets. For some reason it made her feel lighter inside, because she'd heard the worst about her mother, and she . . . Cameryn . . . was still standing.

"You look different, Cammie," Justin said. "Something in your eyes."

With a swift movement, Justin unbuckled his seat belt so he could turn toward her. Reaching out, his hand rested lightly on hers. It was strong, calloused, and warm. "Cammie, I never know when it's going to be the right time, but I've been wanting to talk to you." Once again she sensed the current she'd felt before, like something moving underwater. "I know how hard it's been since . . . Kyle."

"Uh-uh." She shook her head. "I don't want to go there. Did I tell you the dean of CU's forensic college saw me in the newspaper? She e-mailed when she read about how I worked that case. She says I'm a genius."

He smiled, and she noticed again how white his teeth were, how perfectly straight. "You told me."

"It sounds like I may get a scholarship, so it's all good."

Justin pushed his hair back from his eyes, exposing

his arched brows. His lashes, so thick they made her jealous, closed together as he took a deep breath. When he opened them, he looked not at Cameryn but at a point beyond. "That's not the reason I brought up Kyle," he said. "I want to say this the right way." He looked down, touching each of her knuckles with his fingertips. "Before, I tried to say something about us—about you and me. When we worked the case together, at Brad Oakcs's house. Remember?"

"Yeah. I remember." *Oh*, she thought, *here it comes*. Justin had asked her out at the exact moment Kyle had entered her life and she, though tempted, had said no. Her reasons had been rational, logical. At twenty-one, Justin was too old, her father objected, her grandmother threatened to send him to jail, her mother had reentered her life. Now that Kyle was gone, Cameryn was, for all intents and purposes, free. All this played through her mind as she braced herself, half-wanting, half-fearing what Justin was about to say.

"Man, I've run this through my head a thousand times, but . . ." He looked at her, his eyes growing soft with appeal. He moved closer and in that moment, out of the corner of her eye, she saw a blue Pinto chugging past the booth that sold hot chocolate and chili dogs. Inside the car was Hannah, her posture ramrod straight. What surprised Cameryn, though, was the fact that Hannah was not alone. A second person, someone with golden hair, was seated in the passenger side. A girl. Cameryn's gaze followed the car as it turned onto Fourteenth Street before it disappeared.

"Cameryn?" Justin squeezed her hand, bringing her back. "I think I lost you there."

"Sorry. It's just . . ." She shook herself. "Sorry, I'm listening."

Justin cleared his throat. "Right," he said. His face flushed, which made her pulse kick faster, and she was, once again, in the moment. "So, after that day I talked to you again at the Grand. That's when you said you just wanted to be friends. . . ." He paused and Cameryn focused, waiting. Nothing would distract her now.

"What?" she asked softly.

She leaned near him, aware they were sharing the same air, their mingled breath creating the barest of clouds against the window. Outside she heard the Silverton Choir warming up, but inside there was only the sound of his shallow breath and the scent of leather—from his Timberline boots or his leather bomber jacket, she couldn't tell.

Well, why not? she asked herself. Why shouldn't she relax and let this thing, whatever it was, just . . . happen?

Before, Kyle had been a distraction when she'd needed it most, when she'd wanted to escape. But knowing the worst thing, the very worst thing about Hannah, was freeing, somehow. Maybe she owed it to herself to take one more chance, to replace the walls inside her with windows.

She whispered, "It's okay."

"Cammie, the thing is—"

"Deputy Crowley, this is dispatch," a voice crackled over the two-way radio. *"You're needed at the Avalanche on a 10-103f. Do you copy?"*

"Oh, man," Justin sighed. He shook his head apologetically, withdrawing his hand. Picking up the transmitter, he said, "This is Deputy Crowley; 10-65. Over."

"What's all that?" Cameryn asked.

"A 10-103f means there's a fight. I bet somebody had a little too much mead and, well, I am on duty. I've got to go, Cammie. I'm sorry."

"It's fine. I probably shouldn't have sat in here so long anyway. Well, okay," she said. She rubbed her palms along her jeans, her nerves still jangling. "I'd better go, then, and let you get to work."

Opening the door, she was about to exit when he grabbed her arm. "Can we pick this up later?"

"Sure," she said. "I think I'd like that."

He smiled. "I'm glad you're back."

Although she wasn't sure what he meant, a warmth spread from his hand all the way up her arm and into her face. "Yeah," she said. "Me, too."

She watched the police car pull away, this time the sirens blaring for real. Smiling, she waved as it disappeared down the street. Then, jamming her hands into her pockets, she decided to keep walking, threading her way between tourists and townspeople, past the booths and the man juggling snowballs in the air. There was a new lightness inside her. She craned her neck, looking up into the whitened sky. Above her the clouds broke open. Snow fell onto her face, cleansing her, dotting her skin with flakes that melted into water beads. People had gathered around oil barrels lit from within, their hands dancing above the flames. A dog whined, its gold eyes intent on its master's chili dog. The man stood deep in conversation with a woman. Cameryn couldn't help but laugh when the dog, a white husky, reached up to nip off half the chili dog while the man yelled, "Max, no!" *How long had it been since she'd felt good? Too long,* she answered herself. One by one she let her problems go, releasing them like helium balloons into the winter air. She continued east on Greene Street, all the way to Fourteenth Street, and there, less than a hundred yards away, sat Hannah, her engine in idle. The blue Pinto was parked away from the crowd.

Cautious, Cameryn approached the car.

"What are you doing?" she asked, knocking her knuckle against the driver's window.

The noise startled the girl inside, who'd been deep in conversation with Hannah, gesturing as she spoke. Cameryn thought the girl looked no more than fourteen years old. Her strawberry-blonde hair hung in a long braid, and she had on a too-thin blue jacket without a hood. With eyes so pale blue they seemed almost colorless, she gaped at Cameryn.

Suddenly the window glided down. Hannah cried out, "Cammie, this is Mariah. Mariah, this is my daughter Cameryn." The storm that had wracked her mother only an hour before had calmed. She was smiling, laughing, her voice almost giddy.

"Hi," Cameryn said to Mariah. There was something odd about Hannah—her eyes shone too bright, her voice brimmed with false cheer. "Mom, are you okay?"

"I'm fine. Wonderful."

"After you ran out of the Wingate I was worried," Cameryn said, remaining vague because of Mariah. "I don't think you heard me when I said I—I understand."

Tears of gratitude welled in Hannah's eyes. "You do?"

"Mom, it was an accident. It doesn't change anything. All of it happened a long time ago. You should have told me right away."

"Say it again."

"What?"

Hannah's face pinched with emotion. "'Mom.' You just called me 'Mom.'"

"Mom," Cameryn said, surprised how easily it flowed. "So—who is this?" Cameryn's eyes flicked toward Mariah.

Speckles of paint still clung to the back of her mother's hands as she clutched the steering wheel tight. "I saw her at the gas station and I thought, *That girl needs me.*"

"Do you need help?" Cameryn aimed this at Mariah.

There was a tremor in Mariah's voice as she said, "Yeah. I've got to get to Ouray. Your mom said she'd take me, but I'm still waitin'."

"And I will," Hannah explained, each word as shiny as a freshly minted penny, "but when I saw her I knew something was wrong. I wanted to help." Hannah smiled again, like something bursting. "I'm making sure Mariah is safe. It's a dangerous world out there."

By maneuvering forward, Cameryn got her first really good look at the girl. Mariah's nose, small and upturned, reminded her of the pretty dolls she used to line up on her windowsill, the kind with too-big eyes and lips the color of pink roses. Gingersnap freckles sprayed across Mariah's entire face like a honey-colored constellation, and her brows, although unplucked, were perfect arches. She didn't seem like a girl in danger. But then again, Cameryn wasn't sure what a girl in danger lookcd like.

Mariah bent forward so that she could look directly into Cameryn's eyes. "Your mother said she was goin' to Ouray." It was as though all of Hannah's earlier agitation had siphoned into the girl. Clutching her knees so hard her fingertips blanched white, Mariah said,

"We need to be leavin'." She seemed coiled up, ready to spring at the least provocation. In a way, Cameryn could understand why her mother did not want to turn this girl loose. Behind those pale eyes she could sense Mariah's synapses firing wildly as the girl looked from Cameryn to Hannah and then back again. *"Please."*

It was clear Mariah wanted to leave and equally clear Hannah didn't want her to go. The girl's head turned like a ratchet when a group of men, snowboarders by the look of them, walked by, jostling each other, laughing. A truck, followed by a red sedan, slowed before moving on.

Once they passed, Mariah's eyes grew wider. "You know what? I can't stay here." Muttering something Cameryn couldn't understand, she bolted from the car, not even bothering to shut the door. For a moment Hannah watched the girl's retreating figure. Then, stretching across the passenger seat, Hannah pulled the door shut and righted herself, stricken.

"What was *that* all about?" Cameryn asked.

"I don't know."

"Why did you even pick her up? Hitchhikers can be dangerous."

"Not little girls. She was hiding in the restroom at the gas station and she told me she was desperate. I know how desperate feels. I promised I'd help."

"What did she say just now? I couldn't hear."

"She said, 'God helps those who help themselves.' I—"

Hannah stopped abruptly as she stared at the floor, her eyes wide. *"Oh my God!"*

"What?"

"No." The eyes narrowed to slashes. *"No!"*

"Mom, what is it?" Cameryn asked, straightening so she could see inside the car. "What's wrong?"

That's when she saw her mother's purse. The black leather gaucho handbag lay open on the floor. Scooping it up, Hannah dumped the contents on the passenger seat, quickly sifting through them. Her face twisted. "My wallet—she stole my wallet!"

"Are you sure?"

"Of course I'm sure!" With her arm Hannah swept the contents of her purse onto the car floor. "I used my card to buy gas. What am I going to do without money?" She slammed her fist against the steering wheel. "That little thief!"

Cameryn had never seen a person's mood change so fast; it was as if a tornado had suddenly landed inside her mother's small body. "Go and get my wallet!" she cried. "Run! Catch her!"

"Me?"

"Please!" Muscles stretched and pulled on Hannah's neck like cords beneath her skin. "Jayne's pictures are in my wallet! I need them!"

It took Cameryn only a moment to decide. She could still see the girl's bright blue jacket on the sidewalk ahead. As she sprinted, Cameryn's teeth jarred with every step, her body on automatic. Her mother had told her to get back her wallet, and if she could, she would. Hannah needed her.

Over the icy streets, over the dingy gray mounds of snow, Cameryn flew. Mariah had turned west on Greene Street, and Cameryn, determined, followed in hot pursuit. The girl had a head start but had been slowed by a backpack, bulky and oversized for her small frame. Her braid was long, whipping through the air as she ran. Once Mariah looked over her shoulder, and for a moment they caught each other's eyes: Mariah's were scared. Cameryn felt a flash of exhilaration as she registered this fact. She *could* catch this girl, if for no other reason than that Mariah was afraid. She would grab her and reclaim the wallet, and her mother would be proud.

The two of them became like runners in a frieze, with pumping thighs and knifing arms. It was hard pushing through the people. Mariah knocked into a woman, whose cup of hot chocolate flew into the air. "Hey!" the woman yelled, but Mariah kept running. Cameryn, intent on her prey, slammed into a man dressed in biker leathers. She fell so hard to her knees that tears stung her eyes. The next moment she felt the man's strong arms pull her to her feet. "You okay, kid?"

"Yeah," she panted. "Sorry." Her knees throbbed as she

scanned the street. People stood in clusters, their coats and hats as brightly colored as Christmas ornaments, but she saw no girl with a backpack, no long braid of hair undulating. Still searching for blue, Cameryn leaned against the wall until her breathing became even, but she could see only revelers.

Mariah was gone.

Chapter Four

IF ONLY SHE hadn't worn the boots.

Snow had begun to fall harder. The flakes were powdery, like bits of silk. Cameryn hadn't been able to gain traction because of the leather soles on her cowboy boots. Why had she worn them today of all days?

"I want a pair like that, too, now that I'm in the West," her mother had announced on her second day in Silverton. "It's a good thing you didn't inherit my wide feet."

Cameryn grimaced at her own A-width boots, feeling a surge of irritation—they'd made her fail just when her mother needed her.

Ducking around the corner of the Shady Lady, she pulled her BlackBerry from her back jeans pocket and punched in her mother's number, swallowing hard. It rang only once before she heard, "Did you find it?"

Hannah's voice was high, agitated. In the background Cameryn heard a thumping sound, like a pounding fist. "I know it wasn't fair for me to send you, but I knew you could run faster than I ever could. Did you *find* her?" *Thump, thump, thump.*

"I'm sorry. I tried but . . . she got away."

There was a pause. It stretched out so long Cameryn wondered if Hannah was still on the line. "Mom? Do you want me to call Justin? Or the sheriff?"

"No."

"Why not?"

The pounding started up again. "Your father will find a way to turn it against me."

Cameryn tried to reason with her but it was no use. Patrick, Hannah claimed, would find a way.

"I should never have picked her up." Hannah stayed on that loop, chastising herself while Cameryn stood there, unsure of what to do. All the world was frozen: the telephone wires, the whiskey barrels that held summer flowers, the grass, the distant trees. Cameryn began to feel a different kind of chill. There was something off about this conversation. From her forensic psychology books she knew that everyone handled stress differently. Was this all it was—stress? She tried to convince herself, but even as she did, she only half-believed.

When Hannah finally took a breath, Cameryn broke in and asked, "Where are you?"

"In my car on Fourteenth."

"Okay. Let's think this through." As a knot of people crossed by, singing, Cameryn pressed a finger in her ear and turned away. "Did you get Mariah's last name?"

"Just Mariah. I'm sure she's hitched another ride. I'm sure she's gone."

"I can drive up to Ouray and start looking."

"No!" Hannah sounded genuinely panicked. "Promise me you won't go. *Promise me!*"

"Okay, okay, I promise."

"I'll handle this myself. You're a good daughter. I have to go." With that, she hung up.

Cameryn sagged against the wall, the knees of her jeans dark and damp from when she'd fallen. She'd accepted the news calmly that her mother had been institutionalized, because it had been so long ago. But new doubts began to nibble at her mind.

Stop, she told herself. *Think.*

Usually she was able to analyze clinically, sifting and examining evidence as though each fact were a mosaic tile. Line them up in their proper place, and a picture would emerge. But the pieces of her mother made no sense. Elusive, defensive, euphoric, despondent—her mother's emotions cycled as rapidly as the Colorado weather. Punching redial, she heard Hannah's voice mail immediately kick in. Cameryn slipped the BlackBerry back into her pocket. There was nothing more she could do.

With her head bowed, she threaded her way through the throng of tourists. "Hey, Cammie, aren't you staying for the dogsleds?" a voice cried, but she didn't respond, too lost in her thoughts even to look up.

Turning north on Eleventh, she thought how different this problem was from the mysteries she faced in the autopsy room. If it were a body, she would have been fully prepared to peel back the skin and look inside, removing organs, slicing them open in her search for answers. But this was her mother. The mind and its thoughts were intangible, her sharp autopsy knives useless. *The dead are so much simpler than the living,* she decided.

Realizing she hadn't had a thing to eat or drink all day long, she bought a hot chocolate from a vendor and gulped it down. She needed to be alone, away from the prying eyes of her father and grandmother, so she set her path for the library, one block up on Reese Street. Lit from within, Silverton's public library glowed yellow, its light reflecting on snow in rectangular patches. After kicking the snow off her boots, Cameryn made her way up the cement steps.

A small brick building, the library had been built with funds from Andrew Carnegie in 1906. The metal letters over the door were distinct, although the U in the word PUBLIC was shaped instead like a v. Beyond the small antechamber was a second door, this one inset with windowpanes and topped by a glass transom.

A tiny bell jingled as Cameryn stepped inside. Just as she had hoped, no one was there except the librarian, who stood behind a heavy wooden counter. "Cameryn Mahoney, I thought you'd be at the festivities!" Jackie Kerwin exclaimed. Dark-eyed and slender, Jackie was an outdoorswoman who would hike to the top of Kendall Mountain and then, while there, read an entire book. Like many in Silverton, Jackie was a marriage of opposites.

"I've got a paper due and I thought I'd get a head start," Cameryn lied. "I just need the Internet."

"Well, aren't you the dedicated student. You've certainly come at the right time." Jackie swept her arm toward the empty room, palm up. "You've got no competition today. I was about to do inventory in the back, so"—she looked at Cameryn—"unless you need help . . ."

"No," Cameryn answered, relieved she would be completely alone. "I'll be fine."

"Good. Just give a holler if you need me." With that, Jackie disappeared into a back room.

The interior of the library had been decorated like a home. Thick oriental rugs were tossed about on polished wooden floors, while padded rocking chairs filled every corner. A small fir tree decorated with paper snowflakes blinked lights near the front door. In the window Jackie had placed a Hanukkah menorah. Dried lavender and pinecones, in honor of Winter Solstice, stood next to a

Kwanzaa unity cup. Cameryn detected the smell of cinnamon, from the candles, maybe.

But it was the computers she wanted. Two sat atop a long wooden desk, cursors blinking. She headed toward the bright blue screens and, after a backward glance, sat down on one of the swivel chairs. Part of her wanted to get the facts about her mother, while another part of her was against the idea. In the end, the scientific part won out. It was best to know what she was dealing with.

Concentrating, she tried to remember the name of the drug her mother had said she used. As she shut her eyes, she rewound the conversation in her mind. Tregetol. Wasn't that what her mother had mentioned? She hesitated only a moment before typing Tregetol into the search bar, chewing her fingernail as she stared at the screen. The message *Did you mean Tegretol?* popped onto it. When she hit that word, hundreds of sites appeared.

Tegretol was the brand name of carbamazepine, a drug used to treat mania and bipolar disorders. Although she'd heard of mood disorders before, Cameryn had no idea what a diagnosis could mean, and so she carefully typed *Mood Disorders*. This time a tsunami of information washed upon the screen. She scrolled past *Mental Illness Ranked Second in Terms of Causing Disability* to the *Diagnose Yourself* link. From there, she found the *MyTherapy Features*, clicking onto *Mood Disorders*. Following that trail, she found *Bipolar Disorder and Tegretol*. Leaning close to the screen, she read:

Bipolar Disorder is a psychiatric condition defined by extreme, often inappropriate and sometimes unpredictable moods. These moods can occur on a spectrum ranging from debilitating depression to unbridled mania. Individuals suffering bipolar disorder generally experience fluid states of mania, hypomania, or what is referred to as a mixed state in concert with clinical depression . . .

There she stopped. Fear stabbed her as she read the definition a second, then a third time through. Medication promised relief but patients were always subject to relapse. Stressful events, one article stated, were a kind of "kindling" that, when lit, could start a manic fire. Scrolling farther, she read, *A diagnosis means treatment and treatment means control. The compassion of family and friends is critical to a patient's well-being.*

Overhead, chandeliers threw out soft light through glass bells. A stuffed teddy bear looked on from the children's corner. Cameryn didn't know whether to retreat or advance, yet she forced herself to read on. In the comments section, a person with the initials A.B. had written: "*Letting someone in on the truth is the most fearful thing I ever do. Some people look at me like I could hurt them, when the reality is the only one I want to harm is myself.*" Another wrote, "*I'm abandoned to swim against the riptide of prejudice.*" A woman from Texas added, "*For those of you who choose to love people like me, I promise sweet reward. It is a lonely road we walk. The faithful allow us to go on.*"

Cameryn's eyes filled, making the print swim. Turning away from the screen, she sat in silence. Is that how Hannah had felt? *It's a lonely road we walk.* Was her father counting on Cameryn to turn away when she learned the truth about Hannah? She loved her father, and yet she needed her mother, too. She'd rather have this broken woman than no mother at all. *The faithful allow us to go on.* Cameryn knew she could help Hannah while remaining her father's daughter. She could love both her parents, separately, equally. Love meant she didn't have to divide them in her heart.

Time dissolved as she sat thinking, feeling protective. The roles of mother/daughter had reversed: Cameryn would protect Hannah. She would help her mother and keep her well. Now that she understood, everything would be all right.

When her BlackBerry rang she almost didn't pull it from her pocket. It startled her to see that almost two hours had passed. Outside, unseen, the sky had darkened.

"Hello," she whispered.

"Cammie?" It was her father. His voice sounded strangely tight. "Where are you?"

"In the library. I was—looking things up. What's wrong?"

"We've got another one."

She didn't need him to say more. This was an official call. A coroner call.

"Who?"

"They don't know yet. The body's in a lane off of Greene Street. Listen, I know what I said about your mammaw not wanting you to see any more death, but I think I'm going to need you on this one. The sheriff is really thrown. I guess the victim looks pretty young. Are you up for it?"

"Of course."

He sounded relieved. "Okay, then—I need you to go home and get the station wagon. The gurney's still in the back, but I put everything else away in the garage. Grab a fresh body bag. The death kit's right above them on the shelf. The camera is inside on the counter. Gather up everything, then head out as fast as you can."

"Where am I going?"

"The body's in that passageway between the Carriage House and the Highlander Apartment Building. Jacobs said they need a coroner, pronto. You'll beat me to the scene."

Twisting in her seat, she began to pull on her coat. "It won't take me long. I left my car at the Grand, but I'm only a few blocks away. I'll hurry home and load up. Where are you now?"

"I was going to Ouray. I've already turned around."

Ouray. That meant her father had been on his way to see Judge Amy Green. But there was no time to entertain thoughts of the other woman in her father's life. Someone had died, and this time her father had asked for her.

Sighing, he said, "Two people dead in one day. It's too much death."

"Dad, I'm all right," she protested. "Don't worry, I promise, I can take it."

"I meant for me."

The emotion in her father's voice surprised her. He was the one who had told her they had to detach in order to be death's detectives. "The chances of dying are one hundred percent," he'd say. "The only thing to be determined is where and how. If you find yourself getting too emotional, think statistically. We all have an expiration date."

"Dad, what is it?" she asked now.

She heard him hesitate. "Sheriff Jacobs told me—Cammie—this one's a suicide. Some kid put a bullet in his head. An accident I can understand, but taking your own life when you're young and you've got your whole life ahead of you . . . It's just hard to think someone would do that to themselves."

"Oh," she said. She had just assumed this would be a garden-variety death. Like Benjamin, people died in car wrecks. Sometimes they drowned. Mostly they were old and their bodies just gave out. But a suicide?

Her father's voice began to crackle over the line. She knew she was going to lose him soon. The reception from the mountain was spotty at best, especially in a storm. "You know the drill," he told her. "Jacobs can't get—ID until—a coroner—the scene. That—you. Do you think—can work it—a while?"

"Sure," she answered, sounding more confident than she felt. The thoughts of her mother were shoved aside, quickly and completely. There was no room in her head for Hannah. For the first time she wouldn't fill the role of assistant to the coroner, she'd be the coroner herself.

"—hurry. There's—body— "

"I'm on my way," she said, but it didn't matter. The line was dead.

Chapter Five

THE CRIME SCENE: DO NOT CROSS tape was already stretched taut across the passageway, wrapped tightly around gas meters located at the front corner of each building. From her car Cameryn could see a knot of people pressing against the tape, trying to get a better look at the scene. Two teenage girls held their cell phones high, snapping pictures, the flash barely illuminating the brick wall with weak flickers of light while the rest of the town crowded to take photos. Silverton's own, homegrown paparazzi.

Tapping her car horn, Cameryn motioned them away but the people barely moved, reluctant to yield their spots. She hit her horn again, longer this time, then eased the car against the curb and put it in park. Their family's cream-colored station wagon doubled as Silverton's only hearse, which meant that many a person took their final journey in the back of the Mahoney automobile, which was still sporting the San Juan County Coroner magnet from earlier that day. Lyric swore the wagon had a negative energy, a claim Cameryn found ridiculous. She'd never noticed anything more than a faint odor that sometimes clung to the car's interior, which dissipated when the windows were down. Now, grabbing the death kit and camera, Cameryn braced herself for what lay ahead.

By the time she reached the sidewalk the group had swelled to over thirty, mostly people from the festival. It was hard to push through their stolid bodies; the plastic tape bowed in as the people in the back strained against those in front. The tape would break, Cameryn knew, if they pressed much harder.

"Hey, folks, stay back!" she heard Justin bark. "This is police business. Step away from the tape."

The crowd shifted en masse, moving perhaps a foot toward the street. They looked like cows at a fence, Cameryn thought, their bovine faces placid, their necks straining to see over their yellow tape as though it were a split rail.

"Excuse me," Cameryn announced. "*Excuse* me—I need to get through."

"Find your own spot, kid," a man grunted. "We're all here to see the same show."

"I need to get in there. I'm assistant to the coroner."

He turned to look at her. The idea seemed to amuse him. The man's eyes did a sweep to register her long hair and blue jeans, her five-foot-three frame and her pink ski parka with the Gonzo tag. "Yeah," he snorted. "Right."

Suddenly Deputy Justin Crowley appeared, tall and imposing as he lifted the tape for Cameryn, waving her in.

"We've been waiting for you, Coroner," Justin said. Instead of speaking to Cameryn he directed his words toward the man, who immediately took a step back.

"Sorry, I got here as fast as I could," she said as she ducked beneath the tape, her StreetPro gear bag clutched to her chest like an unopened parachute.

"I swear," she heard the man muttered, "they're looking younger every day."

Inside the StreetPro bag were a white sheet, three pairs of latex gloves, a new body bag, a gunshot-residue kit, a dental ruler for scale, paper and plastic bags, shoe covers, medical tape, and a clipboard. Her digital camera hung from a strap around her neck. The plastic tarp she'd spread for Benjamin was still in the bay of their station wagon, beneath the gurney, smooth and shiny. Not a drop of Benjamin had leaked out of the body bag, so there'd been no need to replace it.

The passageway was an eight-foot-wide sliver that ran between the Carriage House and the Highlander Apartment Building. To the south and parallel to Greene Street, a narrow alleyway opened to the back walls of businesses that stood shoulder to shoulder on Greene Street. In order to keep the alleyway clear, snowplows had piled the snow into a towering wall wedged between the two buildings. In front of that icy barricade lay the body, a patch of blue illuminated by a bank of lights.

"She's right up ahead," Justin told her. "Gun's still in her hand."

Cameryn stopped. "She? It's a female? Dad said it was a boy."

"Well, actually, it's hard to tell. We won't know for sure until we turn her over. The hair's short enough for a boy but the shape looks more like a girl to me. That's why we need you here." He put his hand on the small of her back, propelling her forward. "We lawmen can't touch the decedent until the coroner releases it. You've got the power."

"All I need is the photographs and then you can roll her," Cameryn said. "Or him."

"That's the idea."

Although narrow, the passageway was more than one hundred feet long, bricked in on either side by walls more than three stories high. A 1,000-watt halogen work light illuminated the snow so that it sparkled as though it had been salted with diamonds. In the distance Cameryn could make out a figure lying, head toward the wall, its feet sprawled apart at an odd angle. She could see the gentle rise of the back, the blue jeans–clad legs, the tread of the sneakers, and a halo of short blonde hair moving in the winter breeze like seaweed beneath water. It was the blue of the parka that caught Cameryn's eye—the same bright blue Mariah had worn. For a moment she started as the thought *Mariah* flashed through her mind. But blue parkas were a dime a dozen, she reminded herself, and the hair was short, not long and in a braid. Realizing this, Cameryn's heart began to beat again.

Justin stopped her. "What's up? You just turned as white as the vic."

"Nothing. I'm just thinking of the stuff I have to do," she lied, covering up with a barrage of words. "Did I tell you we've switched to using only a digital camera?" Holding her camera away from her chest, she babbled, "The pictures are stamped electronically so you can tell if anything's been altered, which means a digital shot will stand up in court. So that's all I'm using now—no more black-and-white. We just put it on a disk and then we're done. It saves a lot because of the higher cost of regular film."

He watched her closely as she spoke. Justin's eyes were trained on her mouth, as though he were listening not with his ears but with his eyes. "Okay," he said slowly. "Let's do it, then." When she turned, Cameryn's feet nearly slipped from beneath her. Justin grabbed her arm beneath the elbow. "Careful—there's ice." Even through her coat she could feel his warmth.

Halfway down the alleyway, at a doorway, stood Sheriff

Jacobs, one leg propped against a wall. He was interviewing a man who frantically sucked on a cigarette. Although the man's face was passive, Cameryn could see his fingers tremble as he brought them to his lips. It took her only a moment to place him: Barry Leithauser, the cook from High Noon Burgers.

She was about to pass them when Jacobs said, "Cameryn, hold on a tic. Barry, I'll need just a second. This here is official business. This girl is the coroner."

Barry nodded and let his cigarette dangle from his hand, its tip burning red against the brick.

Sheriff Jacobs wore the same clothing he'd worn to the scene of the car crash, minus the hat. The bank of lights illuminated one side of his face. His thin hair seemed to float above his scalp, and his sharp nose and chin obscured his face so that half of him was lost in shadow.

"The thing is—Coroner—you're only seventeen. I'm not so sure you should be working a case like this alone."

"I'm not alone," Cameryn countered. "Justin's with me."

"I meant without your father. I know he thinks you hung the moon, but what you're about to do is official business. From now on, it all counts."

Through tight lips she said, "The coroner told me to start. So I'm going to start."

Jacobs peered over his glasses, his eyes tiny, squinting. "Since you're all hell-fired sure you want to go on, you might want to hear what Barry has to say before you start processing the scene. Give us a recap, Barry," Jacobs commanded.

Barry wore a baker's apron beneath an open parka. His red hair, as coarse as wire, had been pulled into a hairnet that hung at the base of his neck like an old-fashioned snood. There were grease stains on his apron, score-marks. His jeans were dirty.

"Well," Barry said, sounding nervous. "Like I said, I was walking home when I ducked in the alley for a smoke. High Noon doesn't like me to light up—"

Jacobs cut him off with a wave of his hand. "What did you see in the alley?"

"Well, I, uh, I looked down and I thought I saw something strange. I was thinking, *What the heck is that, way down by the snow wall?* So I got curious. I walked closer and there it was. At first I figured it was a mannequin, like maybe it was tossed off from the parade. When I got closer I saw the gun . . ." His voice broke. He stopped for a moment before going on. "I said, 'Hey, kid, are you okay?' Then I saw the hole in the head and the blood. That's when I knew."

"What did you do then?" prompted Jacobs.

"I called 911. The lady told me I had to stay until you guys arrived. She said I wasn't supposed to touch anything. I didn't. I gotta tell you, I'm creeped out by this whole thing." He took a deep drag from the cigarette, and his shaking made the glowing ember dance. "It's freakin' weird. I kept walking around the body thinkin' what a waste it was, killing yourself like that."

The sheriff's eyes were sharp. "So, Cameryn, how does this change the scene?"

"Well, for one thing the area around the body has been compromised," Cameryn answered. "I'll need to get a shot of Barry's shoes."

The sheriff looked at her with grudging respect. "That's right. But the most important thing is the pictures of the gun. Photograph different angles of the vic holding the revolver—take as many as you can, from every which way. Remember to use the scale."

"I'll make sure it's done right," Justin said.

"*I'll* make sure it's done right," Cameryn corrected.

Jacobs made a note on his pad and said, "Start taking your pictures, Cammie. So, Barry," Jacobs said, turning his attention to the cook, "did you see anyone else in this alleyway?"

"No," Barry replied. "Nobody comes in 'cause there's no way out. It's blocked off. . . ."

As Jacobs's pen scratched against paper, Justin made a motion for Cameryn to follow him. Moments later the two of them approached the body. At thirty feet, the blue looked all too familiar and she felt, once again, a flutter of panic. To distract herself she asked, "What kind of gun did the decedent use?"

"A .22."

"That's a pretty small caliber."

"Powerful enough. She's dead. You know, not that long ago, girls used to swallow pills while guys shot themselves in the head. Now a female is almost as likely as a male to blow her own brains out. It's a weird kind of equality."

"Either way," Cameryn said, "dead is dead. But you're not sure it's a girl."

"I'm *pretty* sure. The victim is lying facedown and in that parka, it's kind of hard to tell." Fifteen feet away from the body they stopped. Holding her camera to her eye, Cameryn began to shoot pictures of the scene, the alley, and the churned footprints covered in a patina of snow. Now that she was close, she could see the color of the hair, a strawberry blonde reminiscent of Mariah's shade. The lights had thrown her off, lighting it up to the color of gold, but she could now see the strands of red woven in. Her mind jumped to the shiny blue fabric, the same color she'd chased down Greene Street.

Slumped next to the body's right side was the backpack. When Cameryn saw that, the wind was knocked out of her as though a giant, invisible fist had hit her hard in the chest. The color of hair, the make of the coat, the white slash of sneakers, all were points on a road map that led this body straight to Hannah. There was no doubt about it; this was Mariah, minus her braid.

Justin hesitated. "Maybe we should wait for your dad."

"No," she said, shaking herself. "I've got it."

Snowflakes were stuck to the red-gold hair, unmelted, since Mariah's exterior had already cooled. With rote movements, Cameryn snapped picture after picture: of the decedent's feet, her legs, the rip in her blue jeans, and pictures of the backpack, the gun. After Justin had placed the dental scale next to Mariah's hand, Cameryn took close-ups of the right index finger curled in the revolver's trigger, the palm gently cupping the wooden handle. Clearly, this was a suicide. *What a tragic thing to do.* It was then that Cameryn noticed Mariah's fingernails. They were bitten down to the quick. *Just like mine,* she thought. *I've felt overwhelmed, too. But you can't take it back, because death is forever.*

Edging nearer, Justin said, "Be sure to get a close-up of her wound. Take a lot of those. That'll be evidentiary."

"I know, Justin."

"Just trying to help."

Cameryn focused on the bullet hole. It was small, a bull's-eye on Mariah's right temple, ringed with black. Blood had snaked down the side of her face like a single finger of red. It would have been different, she knew, if Mariah had used a more powerful gun. She'd seen pictures of the damage a .44 left behind. *Maintain,* she told herself. The backpack hunched to one side as if it, too, were dead.

"Now do you think it's a girl?"

"Yeah," Cameryn said. Working in, she placed the

scale against the side of the girl's head. Mariah had obviously been agitated in the car before Cameryn had given chase. Is that what had done it? Had Cameryn's running after this girl pushed her over the edge? Another thought chilled her: Mariah had been carrying a gun. If Cameryn had chased her down this blocked-off alleyway, things might have turned out differently.

She moved the scale to the other side of the body and took another series of shots.

"You think she's a runaway?" Justin asked.

"Maybe."

"I'll interview everyone in town, see if I can get a lead on this vic. Somebody must have seen this kid."

As the camera clicked and flashed, thoughts tumbled through Cameryn, spinning like pinwheels, so quick she couldn't follow their trajectory. Her mother, she was certain, had no tie to Mariah other than picking her up from a gas station's bathroom—one of Hannah's lost girls. And yet in her mind's eye she could visualize the sheriff interrogating Hannah, could hear her father's accusations, *"Do you see, Cammie? Hannah's crazy. I don't want you to have anything to do with her anymore. Death follows that woman."* And Hannah, already fragile, might begin to crack. Cameryn had already sensed fissures running beneath. The accusations, the whispers—what if that kind of questioning sent her mother to her own desperate act of self-destruction? *Why open a Pandora's box? Wait. Just wait.*

"You ever see this person before?"

It took a moment for her to register that Sheriff Jacobs was now standing next to her. For a moment Cameryn imagined Mariah's spirit hovering overhead, watching her tell the lie. "No," she answered. It was only a partial untruth. She didn't know Mariah's last name or where she was from. She really didn't know this girl at all.

"I want to roll her," Jacobs announced.

"Okay, I think we've got enough." Justin was squatting over the body, his hands dangling between his knees, lost in concentration. "I need to clear the gun."

"Do it," said Jacobs.

Gingerly, Justin took the .22 from Mariah's grip. With gloved hands he emptied the bullets from the revolver and dropped them into a paper bag. The gun itself went into a separate paper bag. "Can you initial these?" he asked Cameryn.

Cameryn wrote *C.M.* on the yellow tags.

"Ready to flip the body," said Jacobs. "I want to get a look at this kid. Deputy, on the count of three."

"One, two, three!" The two men gently pushed Mariah over, and Justin pulled the hair away from her eyes. If Cameryn had any doubts before, they disappeared when she saw the face. In death the features were even more doll-like, with her pale, wide-set eyes, the freckles looking not so much like honey now but like rust against the too-white skin. Mariah had already stiffened up, from the cold or rigor or both. Her right hand stayed in position, her fingers still cocked against the side of her head, while her left arm remained rigid at her side. Pale blue eyes had already begun to cloud, as though the irises had been infused with milk.

"Cammie, do you have any idea how long she's been dead?" Jacobs asked.

Both Jacobs and Justin were looking at her, expecting answers. She took a series of short, deep breaths and commanded herself to think clinically. Crouching near Mariah's head, Cameryn placed one hand on the cheekbones and the other on Mariah's chin. She tried to pull the jaw apart, but it barely moved. She then moved it side to side, trying not to notice the tiny serrations on the edge of Mariah's teeth and the blank way she stared at Cameryn.

"What are you doing that for?" Jacobs asked, peering at her over his glasses.

It was important she mirror her father's impassive face, his air of professionalism. Other feelings must be shoved underground. In what she hoped was a commanding voice she said, "There's not much tissue on the jaw, so rigor shows up here pretty fast. She's been dead about two hours. More or less."

"Crowley, check her backpack to see if you can find

any ID. I'll pat down her pockets and search her coat."

It was then that the thought, so obvious, slammed against her. How could she have been so stupid? Her mother's *wallet* would be inside that backpack, or maybe tucked inside a pocket of the blue coat. There it would be, a clear direct piece of evidence linking the two. Like a drum, the thought beat through Cameryn: If they got to Hannah first, she would tell the story about Cameryn and the chase and they would all realize that she, Cameryn Mahoney, Assistant Coroner, had lied about knowing Mariah. That might be enough to make her lose her job. It was now or never.

"Justin!" she cried.

"What the—?" Justin looked inside the backpack. He peered closer, pulling the flap as far as it would go, angling it beneath the lights.

"You got something?" Jacobs asked. "'Cause her pockets came up clean. No ID. You got anything that can tell us who this girl is?"

"Wait, Justin—" Cameryn broke in. "I—"

"Hold on." Justin held up his hand. "I couldn't find a wallet, but I found something else. Sheriff Jacobs, could you come here?" His forehead wrinkled as he stared inside the backpack, as if he couldn't comprehend.

Jacobs clomped over to where Justin stood. The mouth of the backpack gaped open, and Cameryn saw a flash of metal inside. "What is it, Deputy?"

"Look at this." From the depths of the backpack Justin withdrew a pair of scissors. The blades were long, silver, and old-fashioned, with a pattern etched on the handle in a delicate engraving.

"So? Scissors don't mean much."

"Yeah, but check this out." And then, with latex-gloved fingers, Justin removed a three-foot-long braid of strawberry-blonde hair. It hung, swinging like a rope. "Cutting off a girl's hair can be an act of vengeance," he told the sheriff.

Jacobs inclined his head. "How's that?"

It was so quiet in the alleyway that Cameryn was afraid they might hear the pounding of her heart.

"Haircutting can be a sign of retribution," explained Justin, his voice eager now. "When a crime is girl-on-girl, the perpetrator sometimes cuts off the victim's hair."

"Whoa, whoa, whoa, you just made a giant leap there, Deputy. As far as I can tell, there is no *retribution* and there is no *perpetrator*. This girl put a bullet in her own head." Jacobs squinted at Justin while Justin, still holding the braid, stared back.

Finally, Justin said, "Maybe you're right. But there's a psychological aspect to the cutting."

"And you know this . . . how?" the sheriff asked.

"From the police academy. And, like Cameryn, I've read books on the criminal mind."

The sheriff rubbed the back of his neck and let a small

stream of air escape between his teeth. "We're just a small town, Deputy. What I've learned is when you hear hoofbeats, think horses, not zebras."

Cameryn stood frozen. She watched as Justin held out the braid, which now hung limp from his hand. "You're right, Sheriff—this might be a garden-variety suicide. But sometimes the hoofbeats do belong to the zebra."

"What are you saying, Deputy?"

"I'm saying we might be looking at a murder."

Chapter Six

"YOU WANT TO tell me what you're thinking? I keep trying to bring up interesting subjects, but you haven't said three words. I might as well be talking to Baby Doe. That's what I'm calling our vic—Baby Doe instead of Jane Doe, since she's so young," her father said as he down-shifted their station wagon. They had already descended the Million Dollar Highway and were now driving past Hermosa, a small town located on the outskirts of Durango. From the road, the town glittered with bright lights, like jewels against velvet. Cameryn watched it twinkle and wondered about the living that went on inside those houses. In those homes, people were serving dinner and helping their kids with homework, fighting and making up, oblivious to the cargo the Mahoneys carried. Death glided past life, unnoticed in the darkness.

"It's . . . nothing," she sighed. "Just a long day."

"You can say that again. It's like a bloody war zone."

"I know," she said, distracted. "I'm sorry, I'm just . . . thinking." With her head pressed against the glass, she turned Justin's words over in her mind for the hundredth time. *Murder, murder, murder.* If that were true, then she, by not telling what she knew, was withholding evidence of a crime. Suicide was one thing—there was no point dragging Hannah into a mess if she didn't have to. But *murder*? At this point she'd already gone too far. A plunging, hopeless feeling settled inside as she watched the full moon touch the top of the mountain, balancing on a jagged peak like a golden ball.

"Well, let me take a stab at this since you're not talking. Are you worried that Dr. Moore's going to give you grief for being the lead coroner on this one?"

In spite of herself, Cameryn smiled. The "guessing game" was one of her father's strategies to get her to talk when she didn't want to.

"No."

"Are you worried that you haven't finished your application for that forensic guru?"

"No. She's supposed to e-mail me today."

"Okay," he went on, jutting out a thoughtful lower lip, "are you worried about what Justin said—that this is a murder and not a suicide?"

It was enough to wake her from her trance. Pulling

away from the glass, she turned to look at him. "What did you say?"

"Bingo!" he said happily. "If you're concerned whether you covered procedure well enough if the case goes to trial, don't be. First of all, you did a fine job—everything by the book. Are you worried about a trial?"

She nodded, thankful for the excuse.

"But this is *not* a murder. Deputy Crowley was over-reaching."

"Except . . . Justin said that girls cut hair as an act of vengeance."

He smiled to himself. "Well, yes, it's true that some-times when it's a girl-on-girl crime, the perpetrator will cut hair. It happens." For a quick moment he scoped her face before training his eyes back to the road. "But it's *also* true that girls cut off their hair in an act of despon-dency. Obviously, you have to be pretty darn despondent to kill yourself. And who are these mysterious girls that killed Baby Doe? We don't exactly have street gangs in Silverton. No, there was a gun in her hand and a bullet in her head. Far more people die at their own hand than are murdered."

"Really?"

"Really."

Her blood began to flow again as she settled back into her seat. It was true—she'd allowed her mind to dwell on the worst thing it could possibly be, and here was her father, a professional, telling her the case was a suicide. Behind her in the bay of their station wagon lay the gurney. Strapped to it, in the blue body bag that rocked whenever they hit a bump in the road, lay Mariah, her body swaying ever so slightly. Cameryn found the motion, the sounds, unnerving—almost as though Mariah might bc alive inside the body bag. But that was just her mind playing tricks—from cutting open bodies, she knew one thing: dead meant dead.

In her mind she could see Mariah's face and her wide-set eyes that had stared into the falling snowflakes. Her father, once he'd arrived, had been the one to close those eyes. That was the scene her mind replayed—Patrick's hand gently pressing against Mariah's lids while Justin held the red-gold braid.

"I wish we had an identification on our Baby Doe. Jacobs told me they've done a search on missing persons and there's no hit."

"Why call her Baby Doe when she isn't a baby?" Cameryn asked. "She's what—fourteen, fifteen maybe?"

"I told you already, the decedent is Baby Doe because she was just a kid. In my book, that girl's not old enough to be a 'Jane.'"

Although Cameryn understood her father's reasoning, she couldn't help but bristle at the name 'baby' being applied to Mariah. Mariah had been a thief. She'd carried a gun. And yet Cameryn couldn't say a word because officially, she'd never seen Mariah before in her life.

"You know, it's strange that Baby Doe had no ID in her backpack or anywhere else on her," Patrick went on. "Don't you think?"

"Yeah. But maybe she didn't want her family to know—that she was going to kill herself, I mean. Maybe she didn't want to be found."

"Maybe," Patrick agreed.

The lack of identification, Cameryn realized, had been her one incredible stroke of good fortune. Mariah had ditched Hannah's wallet before they'd searched her remains, which meant that Mariah must have tossed the wallet somewhere—in a trash can, maybe. The backpack had been strangely empty, too, another point Justin had commented on. Cameryn hadn't cared about anything except that luck, for now, was on her side.

Her father turned on to Park Drive, which ended at Mercy Medical Center and the small parking lot of the medical examiner's building.

"And . . . here we are," Patrick announced. "It's late." He pulled around behind the hospital to a small red-brick building dwarfed by the towering center. The poor stepchild of the hospital, the Colorado State Medical Examiner Building looked unassuming and plain, almost windowless, in the shape of a rectangular box. "I can't believe this is my second trip down here in one day,"

Patrick said, backing the station wagon close to a metal door. "You know, Cammie, sometimes I hate this job. How about the pep talk—tell me why we're even doing this."

"We do it for the dead, remember? They tell us their stories and we figure out what happened to them and why. Our job is important. We give families the answers they need."

He glanced at her. "If you say so."

"I do."

He tapped the horn twice, and a heavy metal door rolled upward. Ben, the diener, waved them inside the garage. A black man with arms as thick as her father's thighs, Ben was in charge of the morgue's most gruesome jobs. As he assisted Dr. Moore throughout the autopsies, it was Ben's job to x-ray and prepare the decedent, which might include plucking maggots from someone's mouth or breaking the rigor in bodies already stiffened up. At the very end of the procedure, Ben would crudely stitch the "Y" incision, then carefully wash the body before covering it with a white shroud. Despite the grisly nature of his work, Ben usually had a smile on his face. Tonight, though, was different. He looked uncharacter-istically serious.

"We've already got a lot of interest on this case," Ben said by way of greeting. "Police from all over have been calling, trying to see if this here's their lost girl—I got one all the way from Maine. Makes you wonder how many strawberry-blonde teenagers have gone missing. Hello, Cammie," he said.

"Hi," she replied, giving him a tiny wave.

"I got to tell you Moore's a bit on the crotchety side, it being past hours and all. But he doesn't want to wait until Monday to do her, either, since people are yelling at him from every which way. Which means he decided to go ahead and undertake a nighttime chop. Makes for a very long day. His mood reflects that. So, are you all ready?"

He directed the question to Cameryn. Nodding, she went to the back of their station wagon and pulled up the hatch. "Let's get her out," she replied.

"All right then, on the count of three," Ben commanded, and soon Mariah's body got pulled onto the ME's own gurney. Even through the blue vinyl, Cameryn could tell that Mariah's body had turned even harder, like a loaf of bread left out to dry.

Cameryn said, "She's in full rigor. I think it got accelerated because she's so small."

"All right, girl genius, I can feel it, too. But can you tell me what that means?" Ben asked, a twinkle in his dark eyes. "Word has it, you're about to get some sort of scholarship. So tell me what you know." He began to push the gurney up the ramp, his shoulder straining against the thin green cotton of his scrubs. The blood vessels in his arms stood out from beneath his skin as he pushed the gurney to the door. "Are you going to tell me?"

"Why?" she said, trotting to keep up. "You already know this stuff."

"I know *I* do. But I want to see if *you* do." Knocking the door open with his hip, Ben eased Mariah through while Cameryn and her father trailed behind. Then, like a laying on of hands, the three of them found a spot on the gurney to push. They wheeled Mariah down a long corridor past a ficus tree dropping leaves in a corner.

"You gonna tell me?" Ben asked.

"Come on," her father urged, "show him what you know."

"Rigor mortis is caused by the hydrolysis of adenosine triphosphate in the muscle tissue. Basically, ATP keeps tissue soft. With death the body doesn't generate any more ATP, so the muscles become all rigid."

"You're good, girl! 'Cause that's exactly right. So now I'll ask you a second question." Ben turned the gurney an abrupt right-face so it could roll down another dimly lit hallway. "When does rigor start, Cammie?"

"Um, that depends."

"'Um' is not much of an answer," Ben said, smiling. The rubber soles of his shoes squeaked against tile as he stopped the gurney next to a drinking fountain. "Hold up, I'm dying of thirst." As the gurney came to a halt, Mariah's corpse bobbled, and Cameryn reflexively held out her hand to steady it.

"So when does rigor start?" Ben asked, bending over. Outsiders would never understand the way dieners and medical examiners could drink or eat only inches away from a body.

"In as little as ten minutes," she replied.

"Exactly," he said between sips. "And how long does it last?"

"It depends. It depends on how much a person weighs and how much fat they have, and on the temperature and how dry the air is. This isn't an exact science. I think rigor can go for as long as seventy-two hours. And I think the body's at its stiffest between, like, twelve and twenty-four hours."

Ben stood, and Cameryn noticed there was water on his chin. He wiped it away with the back of his hand. "And then what happens?"

Cocking her head, she said, "I didn't know there was going to be a test."

"I'm just doing my part," Ben said. "I'm getting you ready for college. I heard there's some fancy headhunter out for you."

Mariah's elbow made a knot against the side of the body bag. Cameryn felt its hardness beneath her fingertips. "Once decomposition kicks in, the body reverses itself. It goes soft again as it decomposes."

"You get an A." Ben nodded. "No wonder your daddy hired you."

"Yeah, I'm getting a little worried about my job," Patrick interjected. "I think she's gunning for it."

"Not yours," she replied. "I'm gunning for Dr. Moore's."

"You're definitely what's next." Ben curled his fingers around the gurney and said, "Let's get this girl to X-ray."

The casual chatting was the way people dealt with death, Cameryn knew. Like Ben and her father and Dr. Moore, she could regurgitate the facts. But as the gurney moved on the last leg of its journey, Cameryn realized the disconnect between her knowledge in her head and the feel of a human turning to stone beneath her hand. *You never get used to death,* she thought. *Never.*

They passed a room with a spindly fern in a large clay pot painted with Hopi flute dancers. Throughout the building, cheap art hung on the walls, mostly pictures of gurgling brooks and sunrays bursting from behind clouds—she guessed those were meant to bring comfort to the bereaved.

They arrived at X-ray, where, Cameryn knew, Mariah would be filmed through the bag by the machine's long movable arm. "You all know you gotta stay out here," Ben told them at the door. "I'm gonna try to get film so we can pinpoint that bullet. If we find it, we won't have to dig around so much." He wheeled Mariah inside, and the door clicked softly behind him.

Patrick sagged against the wall as if the weight of the whole day had suddenly settled onto his shoulders. The fluorescent lights made his skin appear even grayer; Cameryn could see tiny threads of veins at the base of each nostril. She hadn't remembered seeing them before. There was a redness to his eyes. Squeezing them shut, he pinched the lids with his fingers and said, "I think the day's finally catching up to me."

Just then his phone rang.

"Why don't I go on down to the autopsy suite," she began, but her father held up one finger to signal Cameryn to stop. "Hi, Ma," Patrick said.

Cameryn waited, paying close attention to their conversation.

"We're down here now. . . . With Cammie. . . . We're outside X-ray. . . . No, it's fine, what is it?" His back was hunched away from her, but suddenly he wheeled around to face Cameryn. "All right, I'll ask her. . . . No, I'm glad you called. I'll talk to you later."

Something had changed in his voice. Cautious, she looked up and saw that his face was grave. Her father rubbed the back of his head, then raked his hand forward, making tufts. "That was your grandmother."

Cameryn shrugged. "Okay. So?"

"So she said you never came home, that you left from the driveway and she got worried. She called Lyric. Cameryn, did you see Hannah today?"

Her fingers clenched at the sound of her mother's name.

Guessing the truth, Patrick cried, exasperated, "We had an hour-long ride in the car. Why didn't you tell me?"

"I don't know." Eyes lowered again, she noticed a small

nick in one square of the tile. "I guess I didn't want to get into it."

"Did you— Did you talk about Jayne?"

She planted the tip of her boot onto the notch and pressed it. "Hannah told me what happened."

"She did? Can you please look at me?"

She did. Patrick's eyes were warm, sad, and full of love. There was so much love in Patrick's eyes that it was almost impossible to hold his gaze. But she made herself do it. "I—I feel sorry for Hannah," she said in a thickened voice.

"You feel *sorry* for her. Wow." He blinked hard. "That's not the reaction I expected."

"It's just, there are worse things . . . worse people . . . than Hannah," Cameryn tried to explain. "Baby Doe put a bullet in her head. Imagine how screwed up her life must have been. Maybe she had problems and everyone abandoned her and then she killed herself. I'm not going to abandon Hannah," she told him. "I think I can help."

"Cammie . . . there's more that you don't know."

"But I don't want to hear any more giant revelations. I think I've had enough for one day. Can we just let it lie?"

The door to X-ray popped open, and Ben pushed Mariah out, feet-first. "All done," he said.

For just the barest of seconds, her father held Cameryn in his gaze until, like a cord breaking, he released her. They once again became the coroner and assistant to the coroner, a father/daughter team, the cheerful partners who worked cases together in family harmony. No outsider would ever guess the truth. She wouldn't let them.

"You two ready?" Ben asked.

"Yeah," she said. "We're ready."

They began to walk down the hallway, the worn heels of Cameryn's cowboy boots reverberating along the linoleum in rhythm with the soft padding sound of her father's new shoes. Other than the overheads, most of the lights had been turned off. As she walked, she thought of Lyric and how frightened she would be if she were here. Lyric believed the deceased hovered close to their remains—sometimes, she claimed, unaware they were actually dead. But Cameryn didn't sense any floating spirits here. No, it was the smell that haunted, a reminder of what really went on inside these plain beige walls. As she got closer to the autopsy suite she inhaled it, the sickly sweet odor scrubbed by bleach and covered by ineffective fresheners. The air in the building hung heavy with death. It had entered into the very pores, weaving its own kind of DNA from the hundreds of bodies dissected inside these walls. The hardest thing about her chosen profession, worse than anything Cameryn ever looked at, was this clinging smell of death.

With the ball of his fist, her father pushed open the door to the autopsy suite. Dr. Moore, already at the sink, looked up and grunted. "Didn't think I'd see you again so soon, Patrick," he said. "What's going on in that town of yours? Two children in one day? Silverton's become a charnel house."

"We've had a bad run," her father admitted. With his feet planted, he rocked back on his heels. "Car accidents are part of living in the mountains, but this . . . Well, you'll see. Suicides are always hard, and this girl's practically a baby."

"A baby with a gun. Move it, Miss Mahoney," Moore ordered, turning his small eyes onto her. "Get suited up and get in the game. I don't intend to spend the night here. Since you're our famed forensic prodigy—"

"I never said that," she protested, but Dr. Moore dismissed her objection, waving his hand through the air as if he were swatting flies. "A prodigy should know to get into her scrubs instead of standing there with her mouth open. You'll find them exactly where they were before, in that cabinet over there. Hurry. I've got a job for you. And I think it's something even you have never seen before. Get ready, Cameryn. You're about to go on quite a ride."

Chapter Seven

CAMERYN'S MIND RACED as she put on her forensic gear piece by piece, as though she were suiting up for battle. A pale green gown went on first. Next came a disposable black plastic apron, shiny as beetle wings, the strings of which she tied behind her, then in front, before knotting them together. She lifted a disposable cloth shower cap, the kind she'd seen doctors use in surgery, shoving her hair beneath it so that it ballooned out at her neck. Last, she removed a matching pair of booties to slip on later.

Shutting the door behind them, her father and Ben had disappeared into a back room where Justin and the sheriff stood quietly talking. It felt odd to be alone with Dr. Moore. The doctor had an acid tongue, which made Cameryn apprehensive. It was best, she decided, to say nothing to him until she was spoken to, but when she looked up, she saw something she had never seen before. Words were painted on the walls in a spidery script against a scene of what looked to be mountain peaks. She squinted, trying to understand. *Hic locus est ubi mors gaudet succurrere vitae.*

"Dr. Moore?" she asked. "What is that? What does it mean?"

He turned off the spigot and stared at her, water dripping from his thick rubber gloves. "You're going into medicine and you don't know Latin?" he asked, staring at her over his reading glasses, which had slipped down his bulbous nose.

"The priest uses Latin sometimes in a High Mass, but I never know what he's saying."

Dr. Moore crossed his arms over his ample middle. Had he been more jovial and sported a white beard, he could have been a mall Santa. His white hair formed a wreath around his bald head while his half-moon glasses winked in the light, making him look almost friendly. But Cameryn knew better. Dr. Moore was a brilliant, demanding, work-obsessed man who, despite his prickly nature, she was beginning to like. Still, she remained cautious around him. One time he'd thrown her out of his autopsy suite, an event she never wanted to repeat.

He began to open metal cupboards over the autopsy

sink. "If you want to get ahead in medicine, I suggest you take at least a cursory course in Latin. Most medical names have Latin roots," he told her, pulling out a cotton towel and spreading it on a metal countertop.

"Latin isn't offered at Silverton High."

"Why am I not surprised? It's yet another example of our education system going to hell in a handbasket. Ah, well," he sighed. With his arm, he swept an arc toward the wall as he announced, "That verse can be found in autopsy theaters across the world. Since we didn't seem to have a budget for such things, I painted it myself. The phrase is most commonly translated: *'This is the place where death delights to help the living.'*"

"You're a painter, too?" Cameryn asked, startled. "I didn't know that."

Dr. Moore's voice was dry. "It may surprise you, Miss Mahoney, to realize I have a life outside these walls."

Of course he did—she knew that. But she found it hard to imagine what Dr. Moore did when he was away from the autopsy suite. Squatting, she adjusted a paper bootie, and when she looked up at him from this angle, the man seemed different. The profound grooves that had formed at the sides of his mouth exaggerated both his underbite and his perpetual frown, and yet . . . there was something changed in his eyes. They seemed to be smiling, as though Cameryn amused him somehow. He'd never looked so approachable. Without thinking, she blurted,

"Dr. Moore, can I ask you something? Even though it's personal?"

"*May* you," he said tartly. "I'll decide the answer when I hear your question."

"How did you know you wanted to be a forensic pathologist? My mammaw says I should be a 'real' doctor instead of a medical examiner. Everyone says that."

Dr. Moore pushed his glasses up his nose, staring at her for a moment. "How I got into this line of work is a story I don't often share."

"I won't tell anyone. Believe me, Dr. Moore, I can keep a secret." She pulled on her second bootie and stood—she and the doctor were practically the same height. He might have been taller if his neck had not been swallowed by his generous torso, although his limbs were so thin they looked as though they belonged to another body, as if he were made up of separate parts.

"It's not that kind of story. It's more . . . whimsical." He seemed to be deciding something. "Very well, I'll answer your question. I discovered my path"—he waited a beat, and then said, with absolute seriousness—"from a fortune cookie."

Cameryn was completely astonished by this, and it must have shown, because Dr. Moore said, "Don't look so surprised, Miss Mahoney."

"It just—that doesn't seem very scientific."

"You're young, but as you mature you'll discover that

things—and people—are rarely what they seem." As he talked, Dr. Moore began to busy himself positioning forensic instruments on the terry-cloth towel. "At the time, I was deciding between becoming a general practitioner"—he placed a bread knife on the cloth, straightening it so that it lined up precisely to the towel's edge—"or a medical examiner. I found myself being drawn to the darker art of forensics. So the question before me was to either stay the course"—he set down a bone saw—"or convert to pathology. One night, I took my wife to a Chinese restaurant to talk about which direction I should go."

Cameryn couldn't help it—the words "Your wife?" escaped from her lips.

"Yes, I'm married." He paused to look at her, his eyes fierce as if daring her to speak. "Forty-four years this May. Imagine that."

Cameryn felt herself blush. "Any kids?"

"Three."

"Oh. I'm an only child."

"Which explains your precocious nature, although not your lack of tact."

"I'm sorry—I didn't—"

Dr. Moore shook his head and busied himself with his work.

Overhead lights hummed in the cavernous space, like grasshoppers on a summer night, while every surface gleamed with steel that reflected circles bright as moons.

She could hear the low rumble of voices in a back office and the rustle of Dr. Moore's paper gown.

"It's always better to line up your instruments precisely. I want you to watch how I do this."

Relieved that he wasn't angry, she walked to his side. He was bustling now. She watched as he set down the enterotome scissors, which she knew were for opening the intestines, followed by the Stryker saw, an electric saw used to cut through the skull without damaging brain tissue. With gloved hands he placed a Hagedorn needle, the heavy, curved needle used to sew up the deceased after the remains are put back into the organ-containment bag following an autopsy. The needle flashed at Cameryn like a disembodied smile.

"So . . . what happened with the cookie, Dr. Moore?" she prodded gently.

"Ah, yes, the fateful fortune cookie." Turning back to the cupboard, he removed toothed forceps and a skull chisel, which chimed together in his hand. "At the end of our dinner I cracked the cookie open and pulled out that tiny piece of paper. It read, '*You will touch the hearts of many.*'"

She frowned, repeating the words. "You will . . ."

". . . *touch* the hearts of *many*. Of course that means one thing to most people, but I saw an answer in it. As a forensic pathologist I would touch many hearts. I would hold them in my hands."

Cameryn almost laughed but swallowed it back. It seemed crazy that this gruff man's destiny had been molded by something so inconsequential. And yet Dr. Moore was not only a pathologist, he was also an artist, and in some ways a dreamer. Her eyes drifted back to the script on the wall: *Hic locus est ubi mors gaudet succurrere vitae.* The dead weren't the only ones who delighted to teach the living, Cameryn realized. Dr. Moore did, too.

"Did you ever doubt that you made the right decision? About going into forensics, I mean?"

"Not once. What we do is a calling." He set down the scalpel, which had a longer blade than most surgeons' scalpels, its edge razor sharp. Four blue sponges rested one atop another next to a scale used to weigh organs. Cameryn couldn't help but think of a child's building blocks.

"What's the hardest part for you?" she asked.

"The child-abuse cases, the utter waste of human life due to plain stupidity—that can keep me up at night. But there are compensations. We pathologists solve puzzles by reading the entrails of human beings. We are the soothsayers of our world."

"What about me?" she asked softly. "Is forensics what *I* should do?"

He looked at her, his expression once again sharp. "There is no way I could possibly answer that question. And, although I've enjoyed our little chat, it's time to prepare for the next step." He raised one hand in its heavy blue glove, revealing its palm textured like pebbles on a beach. "Are you ready for your assignment?"

"Of course." Quickly she tugged on her own thick latex gloves, pulling the ends over the paper gown's sleeves to make a seal. "What is it you want me to do?"

His wooly eyebrows raised into his forehead, causing the skin to ripple into his bald head. "You, Miss Mahoney, are going to prepare a specimen jar."

"A specimen jar," she repeated, trying not to sound too disappointed.

"But this is a big specimen. I want you to prepare the largest jar—the one marked '165 ounces.' It's clear, with a lid. You'll find it in that back cabinet there." He pointed. "The ten percent formalin solution is right next to it—the white bottle with the blue writing. You'll also find some precut pieces of string. Grab one."

Curious, Cameryn asked, "What specimen are we preparing?"

"The decedent's brain," Dr, Moore said, sounding delighted. "The whole entire organ needs to be suspended in the formalin so it can harden."

It took a minute for Cameryn to register this. "The brain? What for?"

"So we can put in rods to chart the bullet's trajectory. There's always the possibility of testifying at a future trial, which means we need to cover every base."

"But . . . I thought," she stammered. "This is a suicide. My dad said so."

"Is it? Well, my mistake." The edge was back in his voice as he said, "I didn't know you could render a diagnosis without a full autopsy. Why don't you have your father fill out these papers and save the state of Colorado a lot of time and money? My wife has a roast waiting."

Cameryn bit her lip. "That's not what I meant—"

"Then get out the formalin."

She heard a clunk as the gurney struck the door and Ben appeared, smiling broadly. She could tell from his expression he had overheard the last part of the conversation and was pleased with her assignment.

"Ooohhh, so you're gonna show Cammie how to make a brain bucket!" he cried as he wheeled Mariah into the autopsy suite. "That's a good idea, 'cause the film shows that bullet bounced through her head every which way." To Cameryn, he added, "Dr. Moore's got the best technique I've seen. The last ME just chucked 'em right in a bucket without the string. You got to have the string or the brain settles on the bottom and goes all flat, which messes up the samples. Moore's an artist."

"That's enough, Ben," Moore grumbled. "Go weigh the decedent. And don't forget my music. How about some Bizet?"

"No problem," Ben replied. Then, his voice low, he said, "The man likes his Carmen, as in the opera. I prefer Carmen Electra myself."

"And get the rest of the crew in here," Dr. Moore barked.

Ben's head bobbed in reply. "Right. The sheriff and them are just calling to see if they can get an ID on the girl."

Snorting, Dr. Moore said, "Who are you kidding? They're in *my* office, eating *your* pizza. I saw the box."

Ben shrugged nonchalantly. Patting his stomach, he said, "I always like to share. Let me get that music going for you."

Soon the rich notes of the opera filled the room like incense. Ben wheeled the gurney onto a large metal plate that rested in the floor, which was in actuality a scale. "Ninety-three pounds," he announced, squinting at the numbers. "She was a little thing. Would you write that down for me, Cammie? Yeah, it's that clipboard over there. Uh-huh, that's the one. There's a pen at the top."

"Go and help the man," ordered Dr. Moore, who was now turning on a hose that filled a large, rectangular pan that would be used to rinse off organs.

Cameryn walked past the body bag and tried not to picture the face beneath the vinyl, but in her mind's eye she could see the blank, glacial eyes and the lips slightly parted. What she couldn't get past was the way Dr. Moore had put murder back on the table. Her stomach turned to water while she went through the motions of writing down numbers, her mind once again sifting through facts. What if someone reported that Cameryn had chased Mariah through the crowd? What then? What if the snowboarders came forward to say Mariah had been in the car with Hannah, with Cameryn standing nearby? What if the whole sin of omission unraveled? By remaining silent she had become a cog in the wheel of a deception. She knew the name of the girl who lay wrapped in the body bag, knew of her planned destination. *If it's a suicide, it doesn't matter.* Once, Cameryn had thought that she wanted to be a medical examiner in order to give voice to the dead. But not now. For the first time she was more than glad that the departed *didn't* speak. Hannah needed protecting, and that's what Cameryn was doing. This case was a suicide. It had to be.

"Hey, girl, you're turning a little pale there," said Ben. "Are you okay?"

"I'm fine. Sorry, I'm just trying to focus. Sixty-one inches," Cameryn repeated, entering the number on the autopsy worksheet. Ben was scrutinizing her face. To throw him off, she said, "So, Ben, there's one thing I don't get."

"Yeah?" he replied, wheeling the gurney off the scale. "And what would that be?"

"How could you tell anything about the trajectory of the bullet from the X-ray? I thought soft tissue didn't show up on film."

Ben began unzipping the body bag. Huffing, he replied, "See, Cammie, sometimes traces from a bullet's copper casing fleck off when it travels—that's what happened here. The X-ray of her brain shows little tiny stars everywhere, which means the bullet bounced all over the inside of her skull. One thing I do know, this girl's head is a mess. We're gonna need that brain bucket for sure to tell what happened."

"Does that mean we start with the head first?"

"Can't. She'd bleed out into the body cavity if we did that. We always go in an order. Chest first, head last."

Patrick, Sheriff Jacobs, and Deputy Crowley emerged from Dr. Moore's office, the latter's heavy boots clumping as they approached the body. Cameryn could see a pea-sized bit of pizza sauce stuck to the sheriff's chin. He seemed to be aware of her looking at his mouth, because he wiped it with a crumpled napkin before tossing it into a garbage can. "Evening, Doc," Jacobs said. "Sorry we took a minute in there. We were trying to get a lead on this girl here through missing persons, but we came up empty. Lots of girls are missing, but none of 'em with that long of hair."

"So no one's looking for our Baby Doe," murmured Moore. He had switched his glasses; this pair magnified his eyes so they appeared to glow, catlike. Patrick and Justin helped Ben move the body, still enfolded in a sheet, from the gurney to the steel autopsy table.

"On the count of three," said Ben, and Cameryn could

hear the men grunt as they pulled Mariah onto the perforated metal.

"I'm all set to unwrap her," Ben announced. "You all ready?"

As Justin stepped closer to Cameryn, she could feel the warmth of his body radiating toward her, which helped calm the chill. If she were going to come clean, now was the time. *Just say it. Tell them what you know.* But her lips pressed together on their own, forbidding her to speak.

"Ready," Patrick replied with a brisk nod.

"All right," said Moore. "Let's open her up."

Chapter Eight

"HERE WE GO," said Ben, gently unwrapping the sheet.

The cold, heavy feeling spread through Cameryn as she looked down at Mariah's pale face and the bullet hole in the side of her head. Beneath the bright autopsy lights, she noticed the thickness of Mariah's lashes and the curve of her cheekbones, the waxiness of her skin, the ragged edges of her hair. It was easier when she'd seen her as the enemy. Lying there, Mariah looked more like a victim.

While Patrick checked the body bag, which came up clean, Justin handed Cameryn a digital camera. Pictures got snapped once again, encompassing the ABFO scale that Ben moved from Mariah's head to her elbow to her knee to her foot. Each hand had been placed in a paper bag secured with a rubber band.

"This child is *young*," Ben breathed, leaning close and examining her face.

Cameryn said, "Yeah, I thought you knew that."

"There's hearing, and there's seeing," answered Ben. "I never get used to the kids. Um-mm-mm. I wonder who she is?"

"It's every parent's worst nightmare," added the sheriff, shifting awkwardly in his boots. "You know, I got kids of my own. That girl had her whole life ahead of her, and she did this."

"Perhaps," said Dr. Moore.

Her father gave Cameryn a look but said nothing.

Cameryn knew the drill. There was a rote momentum in autopsies that never varied. She tried to get lost in the checklist, attempted to ignore the undigested secret that sat in her stomach like a stone. When she finished taking pictures, her father asked her to chronicle the inside of the backpack, which she was only too glad to do. Her hands trembled ever so slightly as she unzipped the dark blue pack.

What if Justin missed a pocket with Hannah's wallet inside it? What will I do then? Hide it? Confess?

She needn't have worried. After she opened every zipper and searched each pocket, the backpack revealed only a plastic comb, a ChapStick lip balm (coconut flavored), a small package of Kleenex tissues, and the pair of silver scissors with the etched handles. Each went into a separate evidence bag, which her father took from her, signing and sealing them mechanically. "We'll take possession of the backpack itself when you're done," Justin told her, handing her a grocery-sized paper bag. It was strange, she thought, that the backpack had been so empty. She was just about to bag the backpack itself when something caught her eye. Something was written on the nylon interior. Block letters, printed in ink along the zipper line.

"Dad, do you see this?" she asked, excited. "Right there—it's hard to read because the black ink barely shows. It says 'GILBERT.' Look," she said, pointing.

Eyes slanting, her father peered at the square letters. "That would have been easy to miss. I think you found us a real clue there."

"Yeah," she murmured. "Maybe. Unless she stole the backpack from someone."

Her father looked at her quizzically. "Why would you say that? This girl doesn't look like a thief."

"Uh-huh," she answered too quickly, nodding. "I'm sure you're right."

"At least that gives us a place to start. We'll put that name in the database and see what we get. Well done."

Gilbert. Mariah Gilbert. Now Cameryn had a name to go with the person she'd chased through the street, the girl who had only moments later put a gun to her head and pulled the trigger. Having the surname made it harder, not easier. It made Mariah seem more real.

"Hey, where's her braid?" Cameryn asked suddenly. "It was in here, too,"

It was Justin who answered. Standing next to the sheriff, wearing street clothes, he told her, "In the paper bag on the counter. Your pop signed off on it."

"There was a *braid* in her backpack?" Dr. Moore interjected, clucking his tongue. "So she cut off her hair and put it in her backpack? Very, very odd."

Patrick said, "The haircutting dovetails with the suicide."

"If that is what we're dealing with. You Mahoneys seem to want to jump the gun, pardon my pun." Dr. Moore laughed softly at his own joke. "The word *autopsy* means 'seeing with one's own eyes.' Shall we wait to discover what the body reveals before rendering a diagnosis? Let's roll her. Ben—if you will."

Dr. Moore and Ben flipped Mariah onto her belly, which was a signal to Cameryn to take another round of pictures. There was mud along the cuff of Mariah's jeans, and a tiny rip in the shoulder seam of the parka. Cameryn took more overall shots, and then they flipped Mariah once again so that she was supine. Ben, as gentle as a parent, pulled the hair back from Mariah's face.

"Let's get the bags off her hands," Dr. Moore said. "I'll wipe them for gunshot residue. Unfortunately, a .22 never leaves much of it." With a small porcelain pad, Dr. Moore dabbed the palm and fingers of each hand and dropped the pad into a gunshot-residue envelope, which he then sealed and signed. Next he clipped Mariah's nails and folded the crescent pieces into a tissue, shaking his head as he did so. "The girl's a nail-biter like you, Miss Mahoney. It makes my job harder since there's not as much to work with. All right, people, hair samples are next."

Evidence was gathered piece by piece. With a black plastic comb, Dr. Moore gently raked through Mariah's hair, placing the hairs, plus the comb itself, into a tissue. Once again these were slipped inside a coin envelope. This time, though, Moore handed the envelope to Cameryn.

"Seal and sign," he ordered.

As Cameryn busied herself writing down the date and the name "Jane Doe," Ben held on to Mariah's head. Bending so close that his back resembled a question mark, Dr. Moore plucked more golden-red hairs with forceps, from the front, back, and finally the nape of Mariah's neck. "You say this girl is a stranger to your town?" he asked as he worked.

"Yeah, we've never seen her," answered Jacobs. "It's our Christmas festival, so there were a lot of strangers in town."

Dr. Moore plucked eyebrow hairs from Mariah's left eyebrow. "That'll make it harder to figure things out," he said, folding the hairs into tissue.

"You ready for the clothes now, Doc?" Ben asked as he set the coin envelope next to the others.

Dr. Moore nodded. As if on cue, the team stepped forward to help unwrap Mariah's clothing, piece by piece. The process reminded Cameryn of undressing a doll. Mariah's head bobbed as they removed the jacket, tugging it awkwardly over stiff hands. Inside a pocket she found a pair of blue knit gloves, which she also bagged. Next came the shoes—Cameryn unlaced them, placing each in a separate paper sack. The socks with an orange daisy print encircling each ankle came next, one bag for each sock, the bags labeled separately. The jeans were harder to remove, but Ben tugged at the cuffs, and soon they, too, slipped down Mariah's legs. They were placed in a large paper supermarket bag stamped ALBERTSONS.

"We get them from the store 'cause they work just as well as the large evidence bags, except they're practically free," said Ben, following her gaze as she read the logo.

"This office tries to save where it can," Moore interjected. "We've learned to make do. Lift her up so I can remove the shirt."

Beneath the top was a modest bra, which Ben unfastened with a single expert motion. It looked different from the kind Cameryn wore. This brassiere had no lace or ribbon rosettes—just basic, unadorned fabric, plain and utilitarian. Cameryn couldn't help but be surprised, too, by Mariah's old-fashioned white cotton panties, the kind that went all the way to Mariah's waist and to the top of her thigh. These were the style her mammaw would wear. As Ben pulled them down, Cameryn once again reminded herself of a hard fact: there was no privacy in death.

Dr. Moore placed a small terry-cloth towel over Mariah's hips and pulled out the rape kit, removing long Q-tips and glass slides from a box. At that moment Cameryn could feel a hand on her forearm. It was Justin.

"Come help me log in the evidence bags?" he asked her softly.

"Okay. Sure. If you think they need to be done right now."

"I do," he said.

She understood that Justin was trying to protect her from the indignities of the rape kit. "Here," he said, "I'll read them off and you write them down."

Her mind was divided, half of her writing while the other half was attuned to what was happening to Mariah. As she recorded the bags and coin envelopes, Cameryn listened to Dr. Moore swabbing Mariah's internal cavities, including her mouth. She heard the hiss of aerosol as he applied fixative to the slides and the hum of the blue light as Ben passed it over Mariah's naked body, searching for more trace evidence.

"No sign of any trauma," rumbled Moore.

"I'm getting nothing, too," agreed Ben. Sheriff Jacobs said something inaudible, and her father whispered in reply. She took a quick glance and saw Patrick and the sheriff leaning close, their hands clasped behind them while Dr. Moore jabbed a needle into the intersection where Mariah's thigh met her crotch. The syringe was filled with blood, purple-red, which he once again handed to Ben.

Justin kept his voice low. "They're finishing up the stuff for toxicology. Moore's just pulled blood from the femoral artery. Next is the urine, which means they're almost done. We'll be able to open her up real soon. Whoa," he said.

"What?"

"That is one extreme needle Moore's using—at least eight, maybe ten inches long. He didn't used to do it that way."

She couldn't help but turn and watch as Dr. Moore poked a long needle between Mariah's legs. A syringe was soon filled with urine, destined for the toxicology lab. Cameryn felt a surge of curiosity. To understand death fascinated more than repelled her. The body was a puzzle meant to be read, and Cameryn wanted to read it.

"Let's do the log later," she said. "I want to see."

Justin blinked. "You sure?"

"Yeah. It's just sort of embarrassing with the vaginal

swabs, being the only female in the room. Besides the decedent, I mean. But this is what I want to do."

They returned to the autopsy table just as Dr. Moore peeled open the lids to Mariah's right eye, pushing at the bottom of the eyeball until it bulged from her face. "No petechial hemorrhaging," he said, repeating the procedure on the left. Then, with a sure motion, he took a smaller syringe and stuck the needle straight into the white of Mariah's eye. Cameryn tried not to wince as he removed vitreous fluid, slightly deflating the eyeball. Once again he handed the syringe to Ben, who placed the contents in a tube he capped with a red rubber lid.

"And why do we do this procedure, Miss Mahoney?" Moore asked.

"Because—because drugs show up in the vitreous fluid at a higher level."

"And why is that important?"

For the second time that day, Cameryn felt as though she were being tested. "You can compare the levels of drugs between the different organs. You could figure out if a decedent was, say, *getting* drunk or *coming off* of being drunk. I think."

"Correct," he said, sounding pleased. "My, my—no wonder that recruiter is courting you. What's her name?"

"Jo Ann Whittaker."

"She's a friend of mine. Tell her to call me. I'll give you a recommendation." Tilting his head toward the music, he said, "Appropriately, at this moment you are hearing the jealous lover José singing for Carmen. *'Oui, nous allons tous deux commencer une autre vie, loin d'ici, sous d'autres cieux.'* Roughly translated, it means, 'Let us begin another life, under other skies.' That's what you are about to do, Miss Mahoney. You'll begin a new life in college." Grabbing Mariah's jaw, he gently rolled her head to the side as he bent close to study the wound he swabbed for gunshot residue. Speaking into the bullet hole as if it were a tiny mouthpiece, he murmured, "But there will not be another life for you, will there, Baby Doe?" Sighing, he straightened and said, "I'm ready to cut."

The five of them crowded in—Justin, Cameryn, and her father on one side, Ben and the sheriff on the other. Water burbled like an artesian spring, the walk-in freezer thrummed behind, the fluorescent lights trilled like crickets as they all stood, perfectly still, waiting. Dr. Moore moved to Mariah's right shoulder and Jacobs stepped back as Dr. Moore raised the blade. Then he cut. Starting from her left shoulder, the doctor made a sure, deep incision that curved beneath Mariah's teacup-shaped breast. From the right shoulder he slashed again, until the incisions joined at her breastbone. At the juncture he whipped the scalpel to Mariah's pelvic bone in a classic "Y" incision. Cameryn could see a thin layer of fat, yellow as butter, and beneath it the maroon-colored muscle. She could almost taste the distinctive smell of blood.

"Here's my favorite line from the opera," Moore said as he peeled back flesh to expose ribs. "'*Libre elle est née et libre elle mourra*'—'Free she was born and free she will die.' It surprises people to know I love art in all its incarnations. There is an art to the autopsy as well. I read the color and texture of the human body. I interpret their palette." He folded the chest flap up so that Mariah's face was covered by a triangle of her own skin. Switching to a carpet cutter, he continued to work the flesh free from the sinew until her skin lay crinkled at her sides like an elephant hide.

"Clippers," he said, and Ben handed Moore the pruning shears. Dr. Moore's breathing became more labored as he cut through Mariah's breastplate. Cameryn could tell it was hard work—he squeezed the wooden handles with increasing force until the blades snapped bone. Once it had been freed, he gave the V-shaped bone to Ben, who in turn set it on the table. Reaching inside her chest, Dr. Moore removed Mariah's heart. "Looks healthy," he said. Cupping it between his hands, he squeezed out blood and handed it to Ben. "I'm guessing three hundred fifteen grams."

"Close. It's three hundred twenty," said Ben, and Patrick dutifully wrote it down.

Systematically, Dr. Moore began to remove the organs,

handing them off to Ben to place in a hanging scale while Patrick recorded the numbers Ben called out.

"Do you see how pink the lung is, Miss Mahoney?" Dr. Moore ran his finger down the tissue and invited Cameryn to do the same. "No asthma, no chronic problems. Baby Doe was healthy and young. Here. Feel for yourself."

With a gloved finger Cameryn touched the tissue. It felt slippery but firm, like a saturated sponge. When she pulled her hand away, she saw there was blood on her fingertip. Discreetly, she wiped it on her apron.

The small intestines, large intestine, and appendix were removed, followed by the bladder, ovaries, uterus, spleen, and liver. Finally Dr. Moore removed the stomach, which he drained into a silver bowl, examining the contents like a soothsayer reading entrails.

"The girl ate a cheeseburger and fries not too long before she died—one hour, maybe two," Dr. Moore said, swirling the bowl. "We've got four hundred fifty-three milliliters here."

"Four hundred fifty-three ML," her father said, scribbling the numbers on a sheet while Dr. Moore removed the kidneys. Each organ he "loafed" with a bread knife so that the tissue opened against the terry cloth as though he were slicing a bun. Small samples were removed and preserved in a specimen jar, while Ben, in time with the music, dipped a kitchen ladle into the hollowed remains, rhythmically scooping up blood. He poured it into the sink with the water and Cameryn watched as it disappeared down the drain.

"We're ready for the head," Moore said, dropping the kidneys into a metal bin he'd set atop Mariah's legs. Cameryn knew when the autopsy was done the contents of the bin would be dumped in a garbage bag. The Hefty bag would then be tied and placed back in the body cavity, and then Ben would stitch Mariah back up. There was nothing glamorous about a person's guts. They ended up in a jumbled stew.

Sheriff Jacobs had put on his wire-framed glasses, which made his small eyes seem almost normal. Pointing to the hole in Mariah's temple, he said, "My deputy thinks there may be foul play. What say you? Anything unusual so far?" he asked.

"I say no one can know anything until we're finished. This is a medical examination and I'm not done examining yet. Miss Mahoney, I want you to stand next to me," said Moore. Obedient, Cameryn took her place to the right of Mariah's head. Mariah's torso had been completely emptied. It lay open and exposed, vacant except for the vertebrae of her spine that glinted in the overhead lights like knots on a string.

Dr. Moore put a blue paper mask on, tying it behind his head in a quick knot. The thin gray hairs bristled over the line of the string. "I heard you ask Ben if we could just begin with the gunshot wound to the head, but there is never a variation in an autopsy procedure," Moore said. His voice was muffled. "We go by the book, piece by piece. Put on a mask, Miss Mahoney," he said, shoving a blue paper mask in her hand. "Bone dust is not something you should inhale." She'd been unaware the men had already donned their own masks. The blue paper collapsed, then expanded with their every breath, in and out, like a bellows.

As the opera hit a crescendo, Dr. Moore gave a crisp nod to Ben, who pulled down the flap of skin from Mariah's face, once again exposing her features. The flattened eyes had become even cloudier, as though a storm had rolled in. Looking at that face snapped Cameryn back to reality. What had she been playing at? Before, she'd allowed herself to get lost in the science, but the face brought her back again. This had been a human being. The freckles began at the bridge of Mariah's nose and spread across her cheeks in a nebula that spiraled into her hairline. Someone had loved those freckles. A mother . . . a father . . . They needed to know what their daughter had done to herself, and Cameryn was withholding the answer. She was torn. Her need to tell was so strong the words rushed up her throat, but she held back, wary. *You'll think of a way. But not now.*

"All right, let's see what we can see," said Ben. Balancing Mariah's neck on a block that raised the head five inches,

Ben took his own scalpel and made a slice from the top of the right ear to the top of her left. With an expert motion, he peeled the scalp from the bone while Mariah's head jiggled softly. Then, with strong fingers pushing beneath the loosened skin, he pulled Mariah's scalp all the way forward, far enough to tuck beneath her chin. Strawberry hair puffed at her jawline and swirled past her collarbone. Blue veins branched out like rivers on a map. The back of the scalp was then folded toward the nape of the neck, exposing skull that was as white as mother-of-pearl.

The Stryker saw whirred as Ben cut through Mariah's skull in a line that went first across her brow bone all the way to the back of her head. When Ben put in the skull chisel and turned it hard, Cameryn heard a strange *thwack* as skull pulled from the durum. Another twist at the base, and the skull cap popped free.

"I knew it," said Ben. "You were right, Dr. Moore. We do need a brain bucket. This has gone to mush."

"The formalin will harden the brain so we can test bullet trajectory," Dr. Moore translated. "Watch his technique, Miss Mahoney. There's a trick to all this."

Ben said, "I got to slice it free. See? Now I'm cutting the spinal cord. And if I pull it just right"—he gently tugged at Mariah's brain—"you get a brain out all in one piece. It's just like birthin' a baby."

"Now, hand the brain to Miss Mahoney," instructed Moore.

Cameryn felt her throat tighten. "What?"

"I want you to take the brain from Ben. Hold it carefully and come to the bucket. And for Pete's sake, don't drop it."

Ben's eyebrows shot into his hairline as he asked, "You sure about this?"

"Yes. She wants to learn, and I want to teach."

Cameryn looked at her father, who seemed as surprised as she was. Without speaking he gave her a nod. She understood it to mean the choice was hers. Trembling, Cameryn cupped her palms together as Ben carefully released Mariah's brain into her waiting hands. It was much heavier than she had anticipated, and her arms briefly sagged from the weight of it, but she quickly raised them as she took a step forward.

It was hard for Cameryn to comprehend what was happening. The essence of Mariah was in her hands, wrinkled and flanged, its whirls and grooves tinged by marbles of blood. Mariah's thoughts, her dreams, her memories had been stored in the gray-white matter. Cameryn felt what seemed like an electrical jolt passing between the organ and her own soul. If there was any spark left of Mariah, the ember would be there. *I'm so sorry*, Cameryn thought at the brain, not caring how stupid it might seem. *I'm so sorry, Mariah.* For the very first time, she meant it.

"Come here and turn it upside down," Dr. Moore

instructed. "See this string?" He held it taut across the bucket's rim. "I want you to balance that canal between the two hemispheres right along the line. That's the way."

Carefully, she did. The brain floated in the clear liquid before gently sinking.

"Why are you doing this?" she asked.

"I want to see that bullet's trajectory. Before you arrived, Miss Mahoney, I studied the barrel of the gun. There was no blowback that I could see, none whatsoever. The gunpowder residue around the bullet hole is suggestive as well. Since you lawmen come from a small town, you might not know that in suicides involving handguns, the victim usually drops the weapon or throws it up to several feet away when his or her arm flings outward. Sometimes, of course, a weapon stays in the decedent's hand, but not often. For now, we wait. Come back when the brain has hardened and we'll see what we can see."

"So . . . you think—" Cameryn stammered. She could feel her body go rigid.

Dr. Moore pulled off his mask. His bullfrog neck seemed to swell with air as he said, "I want to get a report on what is underneath Baby Doe's nails. I'd like to see if there is any gunshot residue or any fingerprints on those scissors. It could all come up clean and that will be that. But it's possible your deputy's right." His thick white brows came together, and while he frowned, Cameryn focused on the mark his mask had made over the bridge of his nose, wanting to escape the words she knew were coming next. They came anyway.

"This could be a homicide."

Chapter Nine

"CAMMIE, WHAT'S WRONG?" Justin asked. "You look like you're going to be sick."

"Too much brain bucket, I'll bet," offered Ben.

Cameryn took a deep breath. "I just . . . I think I need the restroom. Excuse me."

No one argued as she stripped off her gown, tossing her latex gloves in the garbage along with her hair covering. Behind her, she heard the murmur of voices discussing blowback on the gun's barrel, and the nicks left inside the skull by the ricocheting bullet. The voices grew softer as the door swung in and out; with each pass she could still hear the words "hard to interpret" and "slaying" until she was too far down the hall to make them out. She thought she'd escaped, but the words trailed after her like smoke.

It wasn't a restroom she needed—just time to think. She went as far as the lobby before dropping into an institutional chair. The chrome frame gleamed in the light, as shiny and cold as an autopsy instrument. She crossed her legs and watched her foot jiggle in the half-light until she commanded it to stop. If she was going to keep secrets, she'd have to become less transparent.

For a moment she stood, and then, with no place to go, she sat down again. The material on the chair was a rough, institutional fabric with an out-of-date, stain-hiding pattern. Cheap magazine tables bisected the rows of chairs. A copy of *Field & Stream* adorned one, while a *House & Garden* lay open on the other. A battered copy of *I Wasn't Ready to Say Goodbye: Surviving, Coping and Healing after the Death of a Loved One* lay splayed on a laminate coffee table. When she leafed through it, she saw the pages were puckered; salted—she guessed, by tears. She picked up the *Field & Stream*, read the cover, and set it down again.

"I would have pegged you as more of a *House and Garden* type," Justin said, surprising her from behind and then slipping into a chair beside her. "You know, cutting, stitching things up." While his arms rested on chrome, his blue jeans–clad legs spread wide, unfolding as if to take up as much space as possible.

"Very funny. Actually, out of these choices I'd have to say I'm more of a *Field and Stream* kind of girl. My mammaw still makes us eat fish every Friday, so for a while I got into catching them. But I don't like to clean fish," she said, wrinkling her nose. It was amazing, she realized, the way she could flip her internal switch and hide what she was feeling. Not only from others, but from herself. "Gutting a fish—that's where I draw the line."

"You want to open up bodies but you're girly about a fish. You are a mass of contradictions, Cameryn Mahoney."

"Yeah. Maybe it's because I have to *eat* the fish. No such problem with the decedents."

He studied her a moment before saying, "If people knew what happened to their bodies after death, they wouldn't die." Justin waited a beat. "Something's happened with you," he said. "I could tell when you had the brain in your hands. That stuff never bothered you before. What's going on?"

"Nothing. I think I'm just hungry," she told him, shaking her head. "I've only had one hot chocolate today."

"What a coincidence. I was just about to see if you'd like to have dinner." He was smiling his Cheshire-cat grin. Justin, at times, could look every inch the bad boy he'd been before reinventing himself as a lawman.

"What do you mean?"

"For a forensic superstar you're a bit slow on the uptake. I mean you're hungry and we're here in the big town of Durango, home of some truly *great* restaurants.

I was thinking of Francisco's on Main. It's only eight thirty at night, still well within the accepted dinner hour in towns with a population of over, say, *ten*. I'll take you home afterward," he said. One eyebrow rose on his forehead, partially hidden by his fringe of dark hair. "Come on, I'll even pay."

"Why?"

"Because I want to talk to you," he said. "About this case and . . . other things."

Cameryn felt her stomach flutter. "Um, I'll have to ask my dad."

"I already did. They're pretty much done in there. He said if you want to go, you've got the 'all clear' from him. Which is actually quite nice, since he hated my guts when I first came to town."

"Not hate. You're exaggerating. He disliked you intensely, but it was never hate."

"Well, here's the thing. When you're at the bottom, there's no place to go but up."

She smiled at this, her first real smile in what felt like forever. When she stood, Justin helped her with her coat, which he'd brought from the autopsy suite. "Your bag," he said, presenting it to her, and soon they were out in the cold Durango night.

"Hold on—you're going to slip in those boots," he warned. When he extended his arm, she took it, feeling silly yet wonderful at the same time. Being this close reminded her again of how tall he was. The snow had stopped falling while they'd been inside the autopsy room, and the sky had opened up to clear away the clouds. Overhead she could see pinpricks of stars struggling to break through the city's glow. When she tipped her head back, her hair reached all the way past her hips. "Your hair is so long," Justin said. He touched it. "Almost as long as Baby Doe's."

"But hers was prettier," Cameryn replied.

"I like dark hair better."

He said this in her ear. A blush rose in her face, spreading from where his breath hit her cheek and moved all the way across her skin. She was still warm when they climbed into his car and drove onto Main Street.

Justin said, "I'm from New York. I can't believe I just called this a 'big town.'"

"Anything is big next to Silverton." Cameryn rolled down the window. Craning her neck, she felt the cold as she drank in the smell of the city. Pungent car exhaust mixed with the odor of fast-food chains. Along Main, she saw freshly plowed snow already darkened from car emissions, as if waves had lapped against it from a dirty shore. She took it all in: the shoppers bustling by, overloaded with bags; lovers holding hands, while fathers herded children. Christmas decorations filled every window. The lights of Durango were yellow, like giant candles, warm and beautiful. She wanted to eat the air itself.

"Shut that window—we're gonna freeze," Justin cried.

"I want to take it all in."

"You're crazy," he told her. "Absolutely crazy." When he laughed, the sound of it rushed over her. She could forget Mariah and Hannah and the bullet wound and her secrets. Justin was pushing the day's darkness from her mind, and if she tried, she could make it disappear. Everything could still work out fine. Worrying about the case until she knew Dr. Moore's verdict wouldn't change a thing. No, she would let herself be carried by this new tide.

He talked to her about a movie he'd rented and his latest passion, extreme snowboarding. She talked about her plans for college. It wasn't until they'd settled into the booth, after they'd ordered their food, that she sensed he was about to say what he'd wanted to in Silverton. He put down the fork he'd been twisting between his fingers. A candle was burning in the middle of the table, casting shadows. "So . . . how's it going with your mother?"

Cameryn, who had been leaning forward on her elbows, pulled away. Straightening, she said, "Fine. Why?"

"I'm the one who got the two of you together. I feel responsible."

"Don't. I mean, my relationship with Hannah is fine."

"Man, talk about body language. You just got totally tense."

To distract herself, she took a sip of water. Setting down

the glass, she waited, her hand crimping the cloth napkin she'd placed on her lap.

"Anyway," he said, "the truth is, I really didn't want to talk about Hannah."

"Good," she said, smiling. "'Cause neither do I. This has already been a hard day."

"Autopsies are pretty rough. Right," he said. Justin looked as nervous as Cameryn felt. He picked up the fork again, twirled it, then set it down. "But here's the thing." He cleared his throat. Cameryn noticed with amusement he was actually fidgeting. "I . . . I did want to talk about Kyle."

The warm feeling she'd been nurturing sank like water into sand. Kyle O'Neil—an Eagle Scout, straight-A student, and football star—had taken Cameryn to Silverton's Hillside Cemetery and kissed her there. He'd also tried to kill her. A sociopath, Kyle had murdered her favorite teacher, and when Cameryn figured it out, Kyle had gone after *her*. Then vanished. No one had found a trace of Kyle since he'd disappeared, even though his picture had been plastered all over the Internet. Fox News had done a report, and Cameryn was interviewed on camera. It was this news piece that had put her onto the radar of Jo Ann Whittaker, the university professor who might offer her a full-ride scholarship. So at least, in the end, Kyle had been good for something.

"Has he been caught?" she asked, tensing.

"No. The FBI had a bead on him in Texas, but by the time they got there, he was gone. It's like this guy vanishes into thin air."

She shrugged. "Okay. He's gone. How much does a snowboard cost?"

"Cammie . . ."

"Look," she said, "lots of girls go out with guys who try and kill them. It happens all the time." She attempted a smile, one Justin did not return.

"Stop trying to turn this into a joke," he said. "This is serious. What happened to you in that shed—when Kyle tried to fry you with that thing—"

"The klystron tube. It was a microwave called a klystron tube."

"Whatever. My point is that attempted murder is a big deal. Some people go into post-traumatic stress disorder from just half the stuff you've been through."

This was not where she'd thought the conversation was headed. "I'm pretty tough."

"But I can see it. It's like you're trying to pretend things never happened when they did. Listen, I checked, and there's money in the victim-assistant program for a counselor. I think maybe you should take advantage of the funds."

It took a moment for her to process what he was saying. "Is *that* what you're doing? You took me out just to make sure I'm all right? You think I'm going mental or something?"

He looked at her, confused. "No. No, no, no. I don't think—It's just—I want to make sure you're okay. I care about you." Her reached out his hand and placed it on top of hers. "Really."

There was music in the background, some Latin number whose notes peaked over the hum of the crowd. The acoustics were muddied by the sound bouncing off the tile that adorned the walls, the floor, even the tabletop itself. Thankfully, at that moment, their server appeared, setting down their food. Cameryn kept her eyes glued to the salad placed before her. Her mind, though, remained on high alert, because Justin's hand was still on hers. She could feel his calluses on her skin, like sandpaper.

When their server had gone, he squeezed the ends of Cameryn's fingers. "I'm sorry," he said. He pulled his hand away, suddenly awkward. Cameryn dropped her hand to her lap.

"I didn't mean to make you angry," said Justin.

"Who says I'm angry?"

"Your face says you're angry. You're pissed that I asked you to go to counseling. Hey, I'd take some therapy myself, as long as it was free." Justin laughed self-consciously. He swallowed, his Adam's apple bobbing in his neck like a cork on water.

"I get it, Justin. No worries. I'll check into it," she lied.

"I can tell there's a lot going on in your head."

"Are you turning into a psychic like Lyric?"

"Of course not," he said. His grin was slightly off center. "But I see things. It's like—when I said Baby Doe might have been murdered, your face went blank. It happened in the autopsy suite, too."

"I sound mysterious." She picked up her fork and stabbed a cherry tomato. "It's like you think I have something to hide."

"Do you?"

"No." Cameryn could look at him now, at his blue-green eyes, a mix of water and grass, thickly fringed by lashes her mammaw said were wasted on a man. Inside, she felt strangely calm. She liked him, that was true, but she couldn't abide the way he saw through her. No one else, not even Lyric, had been able to perceive her soul like Justin. In a way she felt naked. Somewhere deep inside, she was afraid of what else Justin might see. It was wrong to think she could escape from her troubles with him. He wouldn't let her pretend.

Throughout dinner she deflected him with small talk about the winter fair and bits of gossip from town. Try as he might, he couldn't penetrate her armor. When he finally dropped her off in front of her house, he said, "Baby Doe's brain will be hard by Monday. You and I can go together."

"I think I'm going to skip it," Cameryn told him. "I've got school."

"I can take you after, when school lets out. I think this is really important." He reached out and put his hand on her arm. She felt that small jolt of electricity connecting them, thin as a wire.

"Okay. We'll go together."

"Cammie," he said in a thickened voice. "I don't know what happened back there at Francisco's—I was just trying to help. There was more I wanted to say, but—"

"I know. And you did help. Thanks for the dinner. I really needed a break." She reached for the door handle, avoiding his eyes. "See ya," she said, hurriedly getting out of his car.

Her father was already home. She could see his head through the front window, bobbing gently in sleep as he sat in his favorite reading chair. When she opened the kitchen door she heard Justin's engine gun in reverse.

"You're finally back," her mammaw called from her bedroom. "Would you like to come in for a chat, girl?"

"Tomorrow," Cameryn called back. "I need to go to bed. I'm wiped."

"Tomorrow, then."

"Yeah. G'night."

Cameryn climbed the stairs to her bedroom, which was still adorned with pink wallpaper she longed to get rid of. Stuffed animals lay scattered on her bed, and she picked up her favorite, a floppy-eared dog named Rags. The brown eyes stared back, blank bits of glass set above a plastic nose. But Rags was fake, like everything in Cameryn's life. Fake, fake, fake! Fishing her BlackBerry from her purse, she punched her thumb into the keypad. Lyric—she needed to talk to Lyric.

"Hey, sorry I missed your call. Leave a message—peace!" Too tired to leave a voice mail, Cameryn hung up. She went to her window and stared out at the stars that hung from the sky, bright now as Christmas lights. A sky that Benjamin Baker and Mariah couldn't see.

Downstairs she could hear her father's old Simon and Garfunkel song that ended with the words, "an island never cries."

That was what she needed to be, an island, and yet the tears welled into her eyes. There were too many pressures, too many problems. Justin had reached out to her and she hadn't let him. Fear about her mother choked her heart. She wanted to escape but there was no place to go—her problems were inside and therefore traveled with her.

It was then she heard the tiny ping coming from her laptop computer. She'd left it on that morning, and the screensaver had gone to black. Plucking a tissue, she blew her nose, then sat down on her chair and flicked her mouse. An e-mail had just arrived.

I'm in the office working late. I have just received an

e-mail concerning the Kyle O'Neil case you were involved with. I have some questions. Please e-mail me at your earliest convenience. Jo Ann Whittaker.

Cameryn stared at the blinking cursor. The black vertical line appeared and disappeared from the screen, like a tiny, beating heart. Her finger hovered an entire minute before she hit "Shut Down." She watched her computer go through the motions until her screen returned to black. Jo Ann Whittaker could wait. They all could. The problems would still be there in the morning.

Chapter Ten

"GOOD, YOU'RE DRESSED. I made banoffee, so here's a slice to go with your coffee—you need to eat fast, but mind, don't gulp it down. Your father's already gone to Ouray. Mass starts in thirty minutes, so there's still time for you to eat."

Her grandmother bustled through the kitchen in a pair of black knit pants topped by a red sweater embroidered with a Christmas wreath. Mammaw's close-cropped white hair had been tamed with a curling iron, and she'd put on lipstick, a bright cherry to match her sweater. Earrings shaped like snowmen dangled from her lobes, swaying as she set the Irish pie on a quilted place mat. As she dropped a fork beside the plate, she said, "Hurry now. Eat!"

Cameryn walked across the kitchen to slide into the chair. "Thanks, Mammaw. That's my favorite."

"Pure cream and a dash of coffee. The Irish know how to cook," Mammaw answered, looking pleased. "You need to eat, child. You're as thin as a traithnin."

"What's a traithnin?"

"A blade of grass."

Although her grandmother had emigrated from Dublin sixty years earlier, her soul had remained rooted in the green hills of Ireland. Her dream was to take Cameryn there, to the stone cottage in Dunshaughlin where Mammaw had been born. An Irish lilt still buoyed her words, brightening the syllables, and yet it was the only thing soft about her. A thick-bodied woman accustomed to hard work, and a fierce Catholic as well, Mammaw could fire up like no one else. Which would make what Cameryn was about to say that much harder.

Taking a sip of coffee, Cameryn said, "I, um . . . I think I'm going to skip church this morning."

"And why would you be doing that?" Two tight lines appeared at the corners of her grandmother's mouth. With her mug in hand, she sat down on a chair opposite. "Are you feeling sick?"

"No."

"That's the only reason you can miss Mass without it being a sin."

Bracing herself, she said, "I need to see Hannah."

Mammaw raised her chin. Her eyes, pale as Mariah's, flashed. "And why would that be? You were with that woman yesterday, and now you're wanting to play hooky with her today as well? I need time with you, too, Cammie. And so does God."

Cameryn couldn't possibly tell her grandmother all the reasons, so she kept quiet, slowly eating her banoffee so she wouldn't have to speak. The kitchen, a small room brimming with Christmas decorations, smelled like coffee and winterberry, the latter from the candles her grandmother loved to light. Cameryn could hear herself chew as the clock on the wall marked time, every sound amplified in the silence. The swallow, the slurp of coffee, the clink of her fork on her plate—Cameryn ate and drank, all the while avoiding her grandmother's eyes. Finally, she did look up. But the condemnation she'd been expecting wasn't there.

"Mammaw?"

"I've raised you since you were small," her mammaw murmured in a distant voice. "All that time I've fought against that woman and . . . we, me and Patrick, we've been doing our best. It may not have been good enough, but it has been our best. Cammie, we're scared for you."

"Don't be. I know all about Hannah. She explained the accident with Jayne and I told her I understood. We should forgive—that's what Father John would tell you to do."

The lines around Mammaw's mouth seemed even deeper this morning. "Typical. Hannah gave you a cleaned-up version of reality. Smoke and mirrors is what that woman does best."

"But, Mammaw—"

"Listen to me, girl." She took Cameryn's hands in hers. Sunshine poured through the window, the light shadowing the blue veins that snaked across the back of her grandmother's strong hands. "You know about your mother's illness?"

Cameryn nodded.

"Then you understand the woman has always been . . . weak."

Was Mammaw reading her mind? Earlier that morning, when she'd slipped out of bed to look out her window, Cameryn had noticed the way the night wind had smoothed the top layer of snow into a delicate, shimmering crust. From experience she knew that crust would crumble beneath the smallest bit of pressure. As she'd pulled her blanket up under her chin she'd sat, staring out that window, thinking of Justin, her father, her mammaw, Lyric. They all had one thing in common: they were strong. Each of their souls was tenacious enough to stand without help. But Hannah seemed different, needier than anyone Cameryn had ever known. Like that crust of snow—beautiful, yet delicate. It was impossible to walk away from that fragility.

Again Cameryn felt the grip of her grandmother's hands tighten against hers. "You have to understand, we knew Hannah was ill back then, back before Jayne died. We knew she needed help. Your father took her to a doctor. Medicines were prescribed. But without telling us, your mother stopped taking her pills. Instead, she began smoking marijuana as a sort of self-medication. She thought it was a 'natural' remedy. She refused to listen to reason."

"What?" Cameryn asked, incredulous. "But Hannah *hates* drugs. She told me so. The first week she was here she said to stay away from drugs because they were poison."

Nodding tersely, Mammaw said, "Nevertheless. The truth is, your mother got high every day, trying to treat herself instead of listening to the ones who knew best."

The bite of pie turned sour in Cameryn's mouth. Pulling her hand away, she protested, "But Hannah's not smoking pot—"

"I'm talking about *then*, not *now*," her grandmother interrupted. "Please, just listen to the story, girl. You may think your father and I have been too harsh with her, but there is a reason. At the time, your mother's moods got worse and worse, and yet she refused all reason. I suspected—oh, I suspected—but Hannah lied and lied and *lied* to my face. She lied to both of us." She sighed. "In the end, your father believed her, but I knew better. Patrick loved Hannah, right up until that day . . ."

Mammaw faltered. Shutting her eyes, she waited

a moment, swallowing so hard Cameryn could see the faint undulation in her neck. "On the day your sister . . . died . . . your father found Hannah alone inside the house. She was smoking a joint, while you and little Jayne were all by yourselves outside.

"Patrick just lost it. He called her a bad mother. Hannah didn't want to hear it. She jumped in her car and raced out of the driveway so fast she didn't see . . ." Once again her grandmother reached out for Cameryn's hand, cradled it between the two of hers. "Do you understand now? Your father—I—we could never forgive Hannah for what she did. The wastefulness of an angel lost. All because of stubbornness and stupidity."

"Mammaw, I know it was wrong," Cameryn pleaded, "but—it was still an accident."

Mammaw fired up once again. "Is it an accident when someone's *deliberate actions* cause a tragedy? No, no, no—back then, even Hannah realized the truth. The guilt made her try to end her own life, another sin before God to add to the first. And still your father wanted her back, until . . ."

"Until what?"

There was a beat. Slowly, her grandmother shook her head. "No, that part of the story is for your father to share."

Cameryn felt every muscle tense. "Why are you telling me this?" she whispered.

The frown lines deepened. "Because a long time ago, your father lost himself to that woman. I don't want to see the same thing happen to you." Reaching up, she stroked Cameryn's cheek. "I'm just telling you to be careful. You've got a big heart. You need to guard it."

"And you've got a big heart," Cameryn answered softly. "You need to use it."

Her grandmother's eyes widened as she pulled away. The chair creaked as she stood, her snowman earrings trembling indignantly. A crispness had returned to her voice as she said, "When I began this conversation I didn't expect to get your cheek, Cameryn."

"No, that's not the way I meant it. Really, Mammaw. It's just, everyone makes mistakes. Hannah was sorry, wasn't she? We're supposed to forgive, aren't we? I mean, we've been going to church all my life and that's what I learned from you. That's all I was trying to say. Honest."

Cameryn could tell Mammaw was wavering. Finally, with a slight nod, she said, "So you've been listening to the sermons, after all. Well, I suppose you've given me something to pray about. Speaking of which, look at the time! Since I'm needing to say a rosary for the both of us, I'd better go." She plucked her coat off the coat rack and shrugged it on. "Mind you don't stay at the Wingate all day."

"I won't. Thanks, Mammaw. For understanding," Cameryn said, and meant it.

"I'll tell Father John you'll be there next week, no excuses." With that she grabbed her oversized purse and slung in onto her shoulder as she hurried out the kitchen. The door slammed, and Mammaw was gone.

Hannah used marijuana as a kind of self-medication. . . . The guilt made her try to end her own life, another sin before God to add to the first. . . . A long time ago, your father lost himself. . . . I don't want to see the same thing happen to you. The words ran through Cameryn's mind as she let herself into the Wingate, using a brass key her mother had given her. She had thought of nothing else on the drive over. It was clear that her grandmother believed the revelation of Hannah's past would drive some sort of wedge between Cameryn and her mother, and yet, just the opposite had occurred. Cameryn now realized that her mother had not been well. Trying to make herself better, Hannah had paid for her bad choices in the cruelest of ways: with the loss of her child. No wonder she'd attempted to take her own life. The story explained so much—her mammaw's and her father's animosity and Hannah's ice-cold fear. But they had all miscalculated Cameryn's loyalty. Cameryn would stick, no matter what. Some kids at school smoked pot, and she knew the signs, knew the smell, and she was positive Hannah was clean. Since there was no way to undo the past, they all needed to let it go. It was as dead as her sister.

The hexagonal stairs rose up before her and she climbed them quickly. *She wouldn't get lost. It was the other way around. It was Hannah who might drift away, somewhere inside her own head. It was Cameryn's job to make sure that didn't happen.* Knocking against the door with her knuckle, she could hear a choking sound and someone softly blowing her nose.

"Mom, it's me," she said, and tapped again.

"It's open," came floating through the door. Hinges squeaked as Cameryn pushed inside. It looked as though Hannah had been crying. She was half-sitting, half-lying on her bed beneath a comforter, her long hair falling around her like a dark waterfall, rippling and wild. The skin on her face was flushed with two red spots, one on each cheek, as if they'd been painted with watercolor. Instead of a nightgown she wore a T-shirt with long sleeves.

Rubbing her eyes with her palms, Hannah tried to smile, raising herself into a sitting position. "I'm so glad you're here. Come," she said weakly, patting the mattress with her hand. Crumpled wads of Kleenex dotted the comforter like balls of snow. "But shouldn't you be in church?"

"I skipped it."

"Today is a bad day," Hannah said, her voice quivering. "I've read about . . . what happened." A fresh wave of tears streamed down her face. "I can't believe it. That child put a bullet into her head. I hope . . . your running after her—didn't put her over the edge!"

Awkward, Cameryn reached out and patted her mother's forearm. "It's okay," she told her. "If someone wants to kill themselves, they'll pretty much do it. I don't think my chasing her had any effect on her decision." A newspaper was clutched in her mother's hand; gently, Cameryn removed it and placed it on the nightstand.

"Cammie, did you—did you see her?"

"Yes, and I went to Durango last night. Dr. Moore did the autopsy."

"I thought the police would call me, but they never did. I waited and waited for the sheriff to come to my door. Then I knew you didn't tell." When she looked at Cameryn, her eyes filmed with tears.

"I didn't say anything about your wallet. You caught a break, because it wasn't found on Mariah. She must have ditched it."

"I'm scared, Cammie."

Cameryn stood absolutely still. "Scared of what?"

But her mother closed her eyes.

"Scared of *what*? Hannah, open your eyes and look at me."

Like a child, her mother shook her head. "Please, don't tell. I'm so glad you didn't tell." Then she did open her eyes, so wide Cameryn could see the white all around.

"There's a . . . stigma . . . attached to people like me. They never forget. Your father is going to say I'm still crazy and they'll start to talk and I don't want them to talk. I can't stand it when people talk about me."

Pricks of electricity burned beneath Cameryn's skin. The *boom-boom-boom* of her heart beating against her ribs was physical. Then she saw it, a flash, like a fish scale beneath water. "Han—Mom—what do you have in your hand?" Her mother was worrying something between her fingers. Cameryn could see silver metal flash against the light.

At first Hannah pushed her fist beneath the covers, but then gradually, she held out her hand. Slowly, twisting her fingers toward the ceiling, she opened her hand palm-up.

"It's a ring," Cameryn breathed. "Is that yours?"

No answer.

"Mom, where did you get that ring? If it's not yours, whose is it?"

"Mariah left it in the cup holder of my car. She said she didn't want it anymore."

Plucking it from her mother's extended palm, Cameryn peered at the ring's design. The words *Keep Sweet* had been carved into the silver, but not the way a jeweler would do it. The words were rough, etched with block letters.

"Mariah left this in your car? When?"

"After she climbed in. She dropped it in the cup holder and said, 'I don't need this anymore. I don't want to keep sweet.'" Hannah pulled her legs up to her chest so that the quilt made a tent. Hugging her knees, she rested her forehead into the fabric; her face was hidden behind quilt and hair.

"Mom, this is evidence."

She shrugged. "You can give it to the police. I don't want it."

Cameryn felt a stab of fear. She began to pace, back and forth, trying to get her thoughts in a row. "How? How can I say I found it? We did a complete sweep of that alleyway. Pictures were taken. If I tell them the truth, the trail will lead straight back to you."

"What happens now?" Hannah asked, her voice trusting.

Cameryn's mind moved in fits and starts as she sifted through the data, for a moment not realizing that her own hand had drifted to her mouth, pressing her lips as if that could keep her thoughts sealed inside.

"I want to keep this ring," she said finally. As she stood and looked down on her mother's bent head, at the wavy hair, she reached out to touch it. "I've got to keep the ring," Cameryn said again, louder this time.

Her mother's tear-streaked face looked up at her. "I don't care. I don't want it."

"Okay," Cameryn said, thinking hard. "For now, they

think Mariah most likely committed suicide. If that's true then there is no reason for you to get dragged into this. As long as it stays that way, I think it's best to keep everything quiet."

"So you won't tell?"

"Not yet." It was all she could promise, because it was as far as she could think through. "The wallet wasn't in the backpack. It might show up somewhere again. Did you report it stolen?"

Swallowing, her mother looked at her with wide eyes. There were flecks in Hannah's eyes that matched Cameryn's, little bits of gold, proof of the DNA that knit them together.

"No," Hannah whispered. "I haven't told anyone. After you called, I went straight home. I promise."

Cameryn nodded. "In case they find it in a Dumpster somewhere, you have to say you had your purse in your car and you left your car unlocked. Someone stole your wallet and you just didn't want to go through the hassle of reporting it. I don't think it's going to turn up, but in case it does, we have to be ready. We both need the same story. Do you understand what I'm saying?"

"I understand." The knees, which had tented the sheet, disappeared back into the bed. Hannah gave a small smile, a child's trusting smile. "You're trying to help me." It was a statement, not a question.

"Of course I'll help you," Cameryn answered. "You're my mother."

Hannah began to laugh, but then her face changed again as she tried to hold back a sob. With shoulders quaking, she patted the bed even harder. "I'm so sorry. I'm sorry I brought you into this mess."

Cameryn perched on the edge of the bed as a tear rolled down Hannah's cheek to fall quietly onto a quilted rose.

"I have to go now," Cameryn said. She felt helpless, utterly helpless. She wanted to get up and run but instead she made herself be calm. *If it's ruled a murder, I'll deal with it then,* she told herself. Aloud, she said, "Tomorrow I've got to go back to Durango to finish the autopsy. There are some things I need to check out now."

Hannah paused. Once again the expression shifted. She began to pick at a loose thread, pulling a loop free. "They think it's a suicide, right?"

"Dr. Moore hasn't figured out a manner of death yet. Tomorrow he will."

"It's so sad, the way she cut off her pretty hair." As Hannah pressed her fingertips into her forehead, Cameryn tried to quell the sick feeling roiling in her stomach.

"Mom—how did you know about the hair?"

"What?" Hannah's face looked flat and empty, far away, as if her soul hung miles above the mountain clouds. "Oh, the cook from High Noon Burgers, Barry something—he's

Mrs. Kennedy's son. She told me this morning. I guess it's hard to keep a secret in a small town."

"You're right. Secrets never stay buried in Silverton," Cameryn repeated. She decided to believe this. For now, she would trust her mother and everything Hannah said. Standing, Cameryn reached down and awkwardly kissed the top of her mother's head. "Get some rest."

"It's hard to keep secrets," Hannah said, in a voice barely above a whisper. Her forehead wrinkled and her face became soft in appeal. "But, Cammie, if you love me . . . then you have to keep mine."

Chapter Eleven

"WELL, WELL, WELL, Miss Mahoney, you're back," said Dr. Moore. "And you brought your morgue shoes. Your camera, too, I hope."

"Yes," she said. She looked at the floor and was immediately glad she'd remembered to wear her old running shoes to the autopsy suite. The linoleum was riddled with droplets of blood, which created a strange effect; it looked to Cameryn like a red galaxy had erupted on the floor. Dr. Moore's eyes followed hers as she took in the floor. "You missed a messy autopsy this morning," he said. "Ben will be here soon to mop it up."

During her lunch hour Justin had called to tell her he and the sheriff were meeting with some men from the Colorado Bureau of Investigation, an announcement that sent a wave of fear through her. But when Justin added, "Jacobs called in the CBI to help identify Baby Doe—I guess they have some sort of strategy," Cameryn had felt herself relax. The CBI men weren't asking about Hannah.

"As you can probably tell, it's already been a long day," said Dr. Moore. Although it was only three thirty in the afternoon, the strain of the day showed on his face—it was pink, shiny with sweat. The sockets of his eyes had darkened while the veins in his temples visibly throbbed. But it was Dr. Moore's plastic apron that revealed what kind of work he'd been subjected to before her arrival. The apron was streaked with blood, some in vertical stripes, but most lined in horizontal rows that stretched across his chest and belly, each line dotted with splatters the size of quarters. It looked like a musical score, sprinkled with notes from a song. The music of death.

"Is there a problem, Miss Mahoney?"

"I'm sorry. It's just—there's so much blood."

"A drunk ran a red light and hit a pedestrian head-on a few blocks from here. The drunk, of course, is fine and recovering in Mercy Medical. The decedent is already in the cooler."

"That's so awful," she breathed.

"The inequities of death. You have to harden yourself or you'll never get through." He looked at her wearily. "You can put your backpack on the desk along with your coat. Suit up so we can get started, although I don't think you'll need more than a paper apron and gloves. You'll be more of an observer today."

Cameryn dropped her belongings, then walked to the locker and put on a disposable apron. Silently stripping away his bloody apron, Dr. Moore opened a cabinet and threw the garment into a biohazard container marked for washing. The gloves were tossed into the garbage can. He pulled out fresh gloves and a new, folded plastic apron, which he looped over his head before knotting the waist ties behind his back.

"Did you see the sketch of Baby Doe in the paper this morning?" he asked. "The artist did a fine job. He worked off a photograph you took. It was a very good likeness."

"I didn't get a chance to see it yet, Dr. Moore." Suddenly alarmed, she said, "I smell something. Is there a fire?" An acrid odor, like smoke from a campfire, had wafted its way through the autopsy room.

"No, Ben's just cleaning up. It's burn day." Dr. Moore adjusted the loop around his neck so that the apron fit snugly.

"Burn day?"

"Ben's throwing tissue into the incinerator. We do it once every three months. He'll be done soon."

"You've got a *crematorium* here?"

"No. We have an *incinerator.*" He turned to her then, examining her, the lenses of his glasses magnifying his eyes. She could see how bloodshot his eyes were. "At some point we have to dispose of all the parts left in the buckets—heart, brain, lung, liver. After eighteen months, they're gone. Unless it's a homicide. Those parts we keep forever."

"There's a lot of smoke. How much are you burning today?"

"We're losing about"—he thought for a minute, staring at the ceiling—"one hundred and twenty pounds of tissue. It's quite a job. There are regulations on how much we can incinerate at once. Air-quality issues and such."

"Oh."

"Oh, indeed."

Dr. Moore wasn't playing any music. In the background Cameryn could hear the hum of the refrigerator where they kept the bodies lined up on gurneys in a neat row. She'd been in it before. Unlike the storage room, the cooler was thick with the odor of death, almost strangling. Once inside she always switched to breathing through her mouth, even though, until she walked out, she could almost taste those people.

"By the way, Miss Mahoney, did you know my friend Jo Ann Whittaker is the dean of forensics at CU?" He looked at her over his half-moon glasses. "It's very unusual she would reach out to an incoming freshman."

"I guess she saw me on television."

"Do you know she's very connected to the police as well?"

"Yes."

"And how do you know that?"

"Because Jo Ann told me."

It was true. Cameryn had been seated at her desk Saturday night when she'd heard the soft ping of her computer. She'd opened her e-mail. The new message had read:

> Dear Ms. Mahoney,
>
> I was sorry to receive an alert that you have a Jane Doe in Silverton. As a forensic pathologist and dean of the CU College of Forensics, I would like to offer you any help I could provide. I am closely associated with various law-enforcement agencies throughout Colorado. If you have need for assistance in any form, I assure you that whatever information you choose to share with me will be held in the strictest of confidence.
>
> Jo Ann Whittaker

Quickly, Cameryn had replied:

> Dear Ms. Whittaker,
>
> Thank you for your concern. We still do not have the manner of death but should know more tomorrow after we complete a brain bucket. I do have a question about a different case.

She'd hesitated then, because she knew she shouldn't give out information to anyone. Jo Ann Whittaker, though, was the one person she could talk to. A professional tucked all the way in Boulder, Jo Ann would never be able to connect the Silverton dots. Still, Cameryn understood what she had to share would have to be framed carefully. Slowly, she'd typed, *Do the words 'Keep Sweet' mean anything to you? I'd appreciate any information you might have. Cameryn Mahoney (Please call me Cameryn)*

Her finger hovered over the key only a moment before she hit "Send." She had just finished pulling on her nightshirt when she'd heard another ping of the computer. The message read:

> *Dear Cameryn,*
>
> *(Please call me Jo Ann.) Your question will take some time to research, but I should have an answer for you Monday afternoon. Until then,*
> *Jo Ann*

Jo Ann had contacted her again only an hour ago as she'd been driving down the Million Dollar Highway. The ping of her BlackBerry had told her it was an e-mail. Shifting her eyes, she'd glanced at it and seen that it was from Jo Ann Whittaker. Pulling onto the next overlook, she'd heard the engine of her car clatter in idle as she sat staring at the tiny screen, at the same time fingering Mariah's silver ring in her pocket. The e-mail had read:

Dear Cameryn,

It's Monday afternoon and I am, unfortunately, running behind. I don't have all the facts yet, but I can say I have discovered some interesting news about the words 'Keep Sweet' that I think you will find most enlightening. I will share what I know this evening. Can you divulge any more information about the case?

Jo Ann

Although her mammaw talked of God and angels, Cameryn had never really believed in signs. Yet the e-mail had promised an answer and that, in and of itself, was a small miracle. She'd read it once, twice, three times through before looking out her windshield. In a mountain crevice she saw broken tree limbs, victims of a small avalanche. There was a graveyard feeling to that wash of trees; the ones that had died had been reduced to gray skeletons, their arms bleached like bones. Other trees on the edge were leaning, touching, as though the stronger held the weaker. Like Cameryn held up Hannah, she thought. But now Cameryn needed someone powerful to hold *her* up. She knew she'd found strength in the person of Jo Ann. Slowly, on the tiny keypad, Cameryn had written:

Dear Jo Ann,

I'm on my way to do the brain bucket so we'll connect this evening. I really am excited to find out what you've discovered. Thank you so much for your interest and your help.

Cameryn

The thought that someone was on her side had calmed her. As Cameryn had pulled back onto the highway once more, she'd felt the knot inside her relax. What good would it do, worrying and making plans, until she had all the facts? The brain bucket could reveal the death as a suicide; after that she would find a way to get the ring to the sheriff, which meant all the worrying she'd done up till then would be for nothing. Jane Doe's death *had* to be suicide. Cameryn was sure of that. And now it sounded as though the ring would yield an important clue, which could point them all in the right direction.

"So it's Jo Ann, is it?" Dr. Moore said now, breaking into her thoughts. "You're on a first-name basis with the dean and you're only seventeen. It's clear that you, Miss Mahoney, are a rising forensic star. If Jo Ann Whittaker is shepherding you, then you're in the very best of hands. So—are you ready to begin this task?" He gestured toward the counter, and Cameryn was surprised to see Mariah's brain exactly where they had left it. The chemical had whitened the brain slightly, turning it a pearly beige. Picking up the bucket, Moore took Mariah's brain to the sink. "You might want to watch how I do this, Miss Mahoney," he said. "There's a real finesse to the procedure."

Carefully, Dr. Moore lifted the lid from the specimen jar and set it to one side. Then, with both hands, he removed Mariah's brain to hold it over the plastic container while the formalin fell off the sides in a shower of tiny droplets. The string slipped back into the bucket, drifting gently, slowly, until it settled on the bottom like a single strand of hair.

"The brain's hardened up," he said, smiling grimly, "which is exactly what we want. If I had tried to cut Baby Doe's brain before the formalin did its work, it would have fallen apart on the table. Now it's nice and firm. Perfect."

The surface of the brain looked similar to Mariah's intestines, with its fissures and squiggly canals compressed together in a tight sphere. From her books she knew the names of the areas: the central sulcus, the parietal lobe, the occipital lobe, the cerebellum. But the brain was mystic as well—Mariah's thoughts had been contained there, in that wrinkled human organ. Dr. Moore stood cradling the essence of Mariah in his very hands.

"Turn on the water, will you, Miss Mahoney?" he said, holding the dripping brain dead center over the bucket. "I need the water lukewarm. We've got to rinse off the brain before I can start. Make sure it isn't too hot, or the tissue will cook. A brain is surprisingly delicate."

"Okay, I'll be careful." The sink was deep and made of stainless steel. Turning the handle, she adjusted the stream until the temperature felt right. "It's ready," she told him, and a moment later Dr. Moore was beside her, closer than she wanted as he plunged Mariah's brain into the water as if it were a head of lettuce. With a quick motion he took the brain back to the autopsy table, placing it atop the perforated holes.

"Let me get a rod. You get your camera. Ben will need to take a set of photographs, too."

"Dr. Moore?" she asked as she went to her backpack to retrieve the camera.

"Yes?"

Cameryn swallowed, trying to act casual, determined not to appear as nervous as she felt. She removed the camera and came back to the autopsy table to where the doctor stood, waiting. "Did you get any results from the gunshot-residue test?"

"I did."

"And . . . what did they say?"

"The results were negative."

Negative. A stone sank into her chest. If the kit had shown a positive for the residue, the question of Mariah's death being a suicide would be over. It would be proof that Mariah had held the gun in her own hand when she pulled the trigger. Instead, no residue on a victim's hand was a red flag that pointed to homicide. "So," she said, "do you think . . . ?"

"I think it's inconclusive. We're dealing with a .22-caliber weapon. As I told you, a .22 is notorious for its *lack* of residue. So there are no definitive answers there," said Moore. "That's why I'm going for clarification with the rod."

She could hear Ben whistling as he made his way down the hall. "Hey there, Cammie. I'm glad you waited for me. I was doing some incineratin' and it gets *hot*." Today Ben wore yellow scrubs, the color of lemons. Peeling off his gloves, he gave her a bright smile, a smile that was reflected in his almond-shaped eyes. "I hear we got ditched by the rest of the gang. No matter, me and the doc'll teach you ourselves."

"I'm all ready to go here," said Moore. "Let's get on with it."

The rods came in a rainbow of colors, like Pixy Stix, so that, Dr. Moore explained, if they had to track more than one bullet's path they could keep them straight. Since there'd been only a single bullet, he was able to pick whatever color he liked, and he'd chosen red plastic, a long stick as thick as a pencil and blunt at the tip. Cameryn and Ben hovered close as Dr. Moore moved Mariah's brain so that the bullet hole was directly in front of him. Then, with a careful movement, Dr. Moore gently pushed the rod into the bull's-eye where the bullet had pierced Mariah's brain. He worked slowly, carefully. "We couldn't have done this in the old days," he said. "Do you see how I never force the rod?" he asked her, his face so close to the brain his nose practically grazed its surface. "The hole is my guide. Although this looks simple, this is a deceivingly delicate procedure." Finally, he stopped. The rod stuck out a good twelve inches like a single, spiked quill.

"That's it. Take your photographs," Dr. Moore instructed.

Obedient, Cameryn and Ben snapped picture after picture, the light bouncing off the glistening surface. When they were finally done, she and Ben straightened and lowered their cameras to their thighs, like characters in a Western ready to holster their guns.

"Well, looks like you were right, Doc," Ben said, nodding. "Me—I couldn't look at a bullet hole and tell. But this here's just the way you thought it would be. That's why you're the man."

Cameryn glanced from face to face. The cold feeling spread inside her once again. "What?" she asked.

"The rod, Miss Mahoney." With a gloved finger, Dr. Moore touched the rod's tip. "You see it, don't you? It points down. The bullet trajectory slants toward Baby Doe's collarbone."

"What does that mean?" she asked. But before she heard the answer, she already knew.

"It means that this girl didn't do this to herself," Ben said simply.

"Most likely," Dr. Moore corrected.

"Right. See, Cammie, with a suicide, the bullet almost always goes into the head straight. Sometimes, if the vic hesitates, then they kinda flinch the gun, and the bullet shoots right up to the top of their skulls. So when you're dealing with a suicide, the trajectory goes straight across to the other ear or maybe up to the top of the head. But a self-inflicted bullet never goes *down*."

"Rarely," said Moore. "I'll take a few specimens from the wound site, and then we'll loaf the brain. That means," he said for Cameryn's benefit, "that I'll slice the brain in pieces roughly the thickness of Texas toast. I'll be able to precisely chart the bullet's progression."

Inside, Cameryn was shaking. Her thoughts were ribbons now, curling through the air in all directions, but she had to pull them back. She had to *think*. "That doesn't seem very . . . I mean, a trajectory doesn't seem like proof." She held a finger to her own head, placing it to her temple as though it were a barrel to a gun. Angling her hand, she made her finger point downward. "I could do it that way." She was feeling desperate now. Dr. Moore and Ben were looking at her, hard, as if they could see her fear, so she tried to talk more slowly, to take the frenzy out of her voice. "And what about the scissors? Were there any prints on the handle?"

"Nope," said Ben. "They were clean as a whistle. Which

is kinda odd since you'd think Baby Doe's prints would have shown up."

"Except, she could have worn her gloves when she cut off her hair," Cameryn argued. "She had a pair of knit gloves in her coat pocket. Maybe that's why there weren't any prints."

"You make some good points, Miss Mahoney," Dr. Moore said, his keen eyes trained on hers. "That's why, when we're done here, I want to take another look at Baby Doe. Sometimes death reveals her secrets with the aid of decomposition. Are you ready to revisit the dead?"

"Of course," she said, with more enthusiasm than she felt.

When he had finished with the brain, Dr. Moore and Ben headed for the locker, motioning Cameryn to follow them. Her feet felt heavy as she walked toward the cooler. She knew what lay inside: behind that polished steel door rested Mariah with a white cotton sheet draped over her naked body, and next to her would be another corpse, and another, lined up against the wall in perfect white rectangles.

A blast of cool, fetid air hit her directly in the face as she stepped inside. Ben had already lifted up the corner of the sheet to fold it down to Mariah's waist. "And there it is, Doc," he said reverently. "Look at that."

Cameryn took a step closer. The blood-soaked white string Ben had used to close the "Y" incision looked crude against Mariah's pale skin, as if Frankenstein himself had tried to hem a garment. But that wasn't the target of Ben's gaze. He was looking at Mariah's face.

"Well, well, well," Dr. Moore said. "Putrification does her work again. Once decomposition begins, Miss Mahoney, bruising that was previously undetected by the human eye can surface. It looks like Baby Doe was hit on her face, right before she died."

"I think it looks more like a scrape," Ben said thoughtfully, touching the red mark that had spread across Mariah's cheekbone. "Let me check something out."

With an expert motion he flipped Mariah over so that her back lay exposed, mottled red from where the blood had pooled from post-mortem lividity.

"Whoo-wee, strike three. Do you see that?"

Although she didn't want to, Cameryn forced herself to look. There was an outline, a print stamped on Mariah's dappled skin. Like a silk-screen image, she saw the bruise that had appeared after death like a message in a Magic 8-Ball, a finger pointing the way to a verdict she could not accept.

Ben said, "Sometimes an injury to the face comes from someone stompin' on the back. This changes everything."

"It does," said Dr. Moore. "What does that shape suggest to you?"

"A cowboy boot," Cameryn replied, so softly she wasn't sure they could hear.

Dr. Moore peered closer. His glasses had slipped but he pushed them up, impatient. "It does indeed, Miss Mahoney. There's the tip, and there's the heel. Well, it appears we have our answer. I'll have to call the sheriff and tell him the manner of death. It looks like we've got ourselves a homicide."

Chapter Twelve

"WHERE'S DAD?" Cameryn asked. The kitchen door slammed behind her, pounding like the headache that hammered inside her skull.

Her grandmother said, "Patrick's back up to Ouray. And you're late." Although she usually wore slippers, tonight Mammaw was barefoot. Her toes, like her fingers, were as gnarled as ancient trees in miniature, and the soles of her feet made a padding sound as she walked across the linoleum to the sink. Mammaw's hair must have been recently washed and towel-dried. The white ends stood up in stiff peaks from her head, like meringue, and the skin on her cheeks was flushed from the heat of her bath.

Lifting a plate of Christmas cookies covered in plastic wrap from the counter, she extended it to Cameryn, saying, "I think it's getting serious with that lady judge in Ouray, and that's a mighty thing. These cookies are from Amy herself—Pat brought them home yesterday. The frosting's a bit sweet but the cookies aren't bad. At least she knows the basics of how to cook."

"Thanks, but no," Cameryn said.

"Don't be stubborn, girl. The judge is trying to do right by you. She's reaching out and . . . Cammie, what is it?" Her grandmother's eyes filled with worry.

"It's just—they—we—we classified Jane Doe as a homicide. I guess I'm a little wound up. It's been a hard day."

Her grandmother's hand rose to her face. "Another murder in Silverton. Jesus, Mary, and Joseph." Her eyes were wide as she said, "I thought Patrick said the girl put the bullet in her own head."

"That's what we thought at first. But more evidence showed up post mortem. Someone did it to her."

Setting down the plate, her grandmother narrowed her ice-blue eyes. "Does your father know?"

"Dr. Moore said he would call the sheriff, so I'm assuming so," Cameryn told her, hoisting her heavy backpack to her shoulder. "My battery died and I couldn't call. Anyway, I've got homework to do." She felt tired. Bone-achingly tired. Her fear, her despair, her anger—all of it had come tumbling out on that ride home. Before, she'd drawn a line: *If it's a murder, then . . .* But she was no longer willing to honor that division. Mentally, she'd moved the mark further. After all, a ring didn't prove anything—Mariah had left it with Hannah of her own accord. Hannah's mental illness didn't prove anything—there were millions of people with bipolar disorder. She wanted to be in her room, alone, so that she could read the articles she'd printed, then stashed, on her mother's illness. "The Role of Family and Friends in a Bipolar Person's Life" was neatly tucked between her mattress and box springs.

"Before you go hiding upstairs you should know they think they've discovered who she is," Mammaw said.

The breath sucked back in Cameryn's throat as she asked, "What are you talking about? For Baby Doe? They've got a name?"

"It was an anonymous tip. Someone gave the real name of Baby Doe, told where she lived, and hung up"—Mammaw snapped her fingers—"just like that. The sheriff confirmed it."

"So who is Baby Doe?" Cameryn demanded.

"I don't remember. Ask your father. The point is, they found her, and that's a blessing. My gracious," she exclaimed. "Someone's driving up and I've got nothing but a robe on. Get the door, Cammie. If I'm not mistaken, the visitor is your Justin Crowley."

"He's not *my* Justin Crowley," she muttered, but her grandmother had already escaped up the stairs. In spite of herself, Cameryn finger-combed her hair. When she pulled open the door, the plastic lighted wreath rocked on its hook.

"Cameryn, I'm glad you're home," Justin told her. He had on boots with heels so thick his head almost touched the top of the doorframe. Although the evening was cold, he wore no hat, and the tips of his ears flamed red. Usually there was an easiness about Justin, but tonight he stood stiffly. His dark brows met in the center, and his eyes were no longer greenish blue but indigo, like the sky before a storm.

"Justin," she said, "come in."

"Is anyone else home?"

"Just my grandmother."

"Then I'll stay here."

"Why?" Apprehension spread through her as she looked at Justin's face. Whatever he wanted to tell her, it was bad news.

"Can you step outside, just for a minute? It's important—Cammie, I want to keep this private."

Shrugging, she said, "Sure."

"This won't take long. It's just two things."

As he spoke, his breath blew into the air in a warm cloud, dissipating before it reached her. But she could smell it. Peppermint, from a Tic Tac, she guessed, hiding somewhere in the back of his mouth. A shock of dark hair had fallen into his eyes; for once, he left it there.

She stepped onto the cement, pulling the door shut behind her. There was only three feet of space, and

Justin had barely moved. They were too close, no more than ten inches apart. The lights on the wreath blinked on and off; she watched him in the flickering glow.

He cleared his throat. "The vic's real name is Esther Childs."

"*Esther Childs?*" Cameryn felt her eyes go wide. "Are you sure that's right? How do you know that's her name?"

"We got a tip. A lady from Durango. She called from a phone booth at the Loaf 'N Jug on Sixth Street. She wouldn't say who she was. Why do you look so surprised, Cammie? Do you know something you're not telling me?"

"Of course not." Evasive, Cameryn stared at the edge of his collar, trying to keep from returning his gaze. "Why do you think she wanted to stay anonymous?"

"Who knows?" He shrugged. "Some people don't like to get involved. Anyway, we sent a picture of the vic to a sheriff in Arizona and they ran it down to the Childs family. The family made a positive ID. Cameryn, they're a wreck—Jacobs told me the family lost it when they found out it was a homicide. The Childses are demanding answers, and so far we don't have any." Justin placed his palm on the siding of the house, close to her head.

"Okay," she said. "Great. Now we know who she is. So what was the other thing?"

Justin hesitated. Cameryn's spine was pressed against the door, and he wasn't moving back like she thought he would. She could feel his heat radiating toward her and hers toward him, like two auras bumping into each other, creating an energy all its own. Thrusting her hands into her pockets, she waited.

"What's the other thing?" she asked again.

"Do you know Willie Wheeler? He's the man who runs the gift shop on Eleventh."

"Yeah." Cameryn nodded. "I know him. If you live in Silverton you end up knowing everybody."

"Willie Wheeler called the station today. He read the article in the paper and saw the sketch. He had some information."

"He did?"

"I took the report. Willie said—he said he saw your mother with the decedent. He said he saw Hannah and Esther talking in Hannah's car the day Esther's body was found." Justin narrowed his eyes. "Do you know anything about that?"

Cameryn could not respond. She stood, frozen, her back as cold as the siding on the house.

"This is serious. The case has been bumped up to a homicide investigation. Your mother needs to come forward and say what she knows. You've been spending a lot of time with Hannah lately. Did she tell you she met this girl?"

There was nothing Cameryn wanted more than to escape. Hannah, so flighty and distracted, could very well crack under Justin's questioning. She might tell about the "Keep Sweet" ring. The ring Cameryn carried in her pocket. Or the wallet. The wallet she'd chased and lied about.

"Cameryn, are you listening to me? I'm asking you direct: Did your mother say anything at all to you about meeting Esther?"

Her head, as if on its own accord, shook *no*.

"You're sure," Justin pressed. "You're *absolutely* sure."

Cameryn nodded. Now she was lying to Justin. One lie on top of another, like stones, so many, so large they'd turned into a wall.

"I already went to the Wingate but Hannah wasn't there. I've called but she hasn't picked up. Do you know where she is?"

This she could answer truthfully. "No. I had school and then the brain bucket and I just got home. The battery on my BlackBerry died—if Hannah tried to reach me, I didn't get the message." Focus on the lights, the blinking colors on his face. Not on the cracks that were breaking inside her. She could feel them spreading, like a foundation rocked by an earthquake. If she didn't take control, these fissures would make her crumble.

For an instant Cameryn closed her eyes, aware of the ring in her pocket, small and round. When she opened them, she could see Justin and his look of disbelief. He stared, his eyes dark in the half-light. Cameryn made herself look back.

"All right," he said at last. "Then we'll leave it at that." He dropped his arm and stepped away, freeing her. "If you hear from Hannah, tell her I need to talk to her," he said, sounding as though he was sorry he came. Well, she was sorry, too. Everything had started to spin out of control, and she didn't know how to pull it back.

"Good night, Cameryn." Justin jumped down the last two stairs. Soon his engine roared to life and he was backing out, his headlights sweeping across their lawn as he pulled onto the street. His taillights lit up like angry red eyes, and he was gone.

Numb, she went inside the kitchen. Her grand-mother was making small sounds from her room, getting dressed, Cameryn figured. By stepping only on the edges of the stairs where they wouldn't squeak, Cameryn made her way quietly to her own bedroom, silently, carefully, so as not to alert her mammaw, who might still want to talk. She didn't turn on the lights as she stepped inside, guided by the glow from her screensaver. Fish swam in the computer screen's artificial water, moving through the underwater light.

She flopped onto her bed, burying her face into her pillow. Pain, already seeping through her soul, burst through the wall in her heart. *There was a witness.* The very thing she'd been afraid of had happened. Things had turned even more complicated and would only get worse. It was time, she knew, for her mother to come forward, because the noose was tightening inch by inch. She would have to talk her mother into it.

Pulling her phone from its cradle, Cameryn punched in her mother's number, but immediately Hannah's voice message came on. Cameryn hung up, unsure of what to do next. She thought of the articles on bipolar disorder beneath her bed, but was too tired to read them. She was too tired to think, too tired to force her mind to wake up and calculate the worst possible outcome of each choice available. The witness, the brain bucket, and the word *murder* swirled through her head in a sick kaleidoscope. There was nowhere to turn, nothing to do.

Two notes chimed from her computer telling her an e-mail had arrived. As though she were moving underwater, Cameryn made her way to her desk. It was a message from Jo Ann:

> *Cameryn,*
>
> *I called my friend at the bureau and discovered there is quite a history to the words "Keep Sweet." Keep Sweet is a saying used by Fundamentalist Mormons. These Fundamentalists are an offshoot and <u>are not</u> part of the mainstream Church of Jesus Christ of Latter Day Saints. They absolutely do not belong to the real Mormon Church—it's important to make that distinction. The Fundamentalists believe in something called "the Principle"—which means*

that a man must marry at least three wives in order to enter their highest heaven, the Celestial Kingdom. According to my friend, "Keep Sweet" is part of a slogan that also says, "perfect obedience brings perfect faith." This saying is aimed exclusively at girls.

It sounds as though the Fundamentalist life, especially for the women, is a hard one. At a very young age the girls undergo something called "The Placement." The Placement is done by their Prophet, who is whichever man is currently ruling over his people. Girls as young as twelve are married off to old men. Young boys are sent away at puberty—often called the "lost boys" because they are taken from their community and left to fend for themselves. (Obviously, the older men must get rid of the younger males, since only a few men have all the women.) Although it varies by community, some rules are exceedingly harsh. There have been reports of severe abuse, but it is difficult if not impossible to track this, since the Fundamentalists live in towns that are closed to outsiders. Does the term "Keep Sweet" involve a forensic case you're working on?

I hope this information is of help. I look forward to hearing from you.

Jo Ann Whittaker

A thought electrified Cameryn as she grabbed her phone and punched in her mother's number once again.

Pick up, pick up, pick up! she commanded.

"Hello?"

"Mom! It's me Cameryn. Are you home?"

"Yes."

"Stay there. I have something important to tell you. We have to talk and I'm coming over right now. Mom, I think I know who killed Mariah!"

Chapter Thirteen

MRS. KENNEDY, THE owner of the Wingate, was in the parlor reading a book when Cameryn let herself in.

"Your mother's popular this evening. She's already got a visitor. Go right on up."

"Who's with her?" Cameryn asked.

"Would you like some tea?" Mrs. Kennedy deflected the question. "I was just making—"

"No," Cameryn said. "I'm fine." She took off her coat and hung it on a brass coat rack as a high-pitched whistle came from the kitchen.

"And there's my water boiling. Let me know if you change your mind." She left Cameryn, humming to herself as she disappeared around a corner.

Who was in the room with her mother? Cameryn, who had been bursting with good news, held back. Quiet, she went up the stairs. The door to Hannah's room was ajar, and she could see Hannah perched in the wingback chair wearing a pair of jeans and a too-large sweater that bunched in her lap. Her hair hung in tousled curls and her feet were bare. For a moment, Cameryn stared. Hannah's face had delicate, straight bones and wide, dark eyes— Cameryn's eyes. The eyes, though, looked frightened.

"I don't know. I don't remember," Hannah was repeating, over and over.

"I'm just asking—have you been taking your Tegretol?" It was a male voice, and familiar. When Cameryn heard it, her heart sank.

"I think so," said Hannah, sounding like a child. "But I don't remember for sure."

"Hannah, you're going into a manic phase. You may not be able to tell, but I can. You're talking nonstop."

"No, Justin, I've never been better. Cameryn thinks I'm fine."

"She didn't know you in New York. I did. Show me your prescriptions. Or do you even have them?"

Trapped in the hallway, Cameryn stood perfectly still. She watched her mother rise and go out of her line of sight and then return, dropping two bottles into Justin's hands.

"There. See? Here they are. Are you satisfied, Justin? I've got my medicine."

All the lights were on, both the overhead and the squat

bedside lamp centered on an end table. A light in the bathroom cast a fan-shaped glow onto the carpet. Her mother's voice lost its wispiness. "This is none of your business."

From where Cameryn stood, all she could see of Justin were his hands. She watched as he popped a lid, spilling the contents onto his palm. "The Tegretol," he said. The pills were white ovals, which he then replaced. "And the Fluoxetine." These were a deeper pink tablet, shaped like jelly beans. "Both of these are full. Look at the date—Hannah, you haven't taken a single pill since you came here," he accused. "Is that why you've been hiding from me?"

"I'm not hiding. I've just been busy."

"You can't stop taking your pills. You know better."

She dropped back into the chair. "Those *pills* make me feel flat. It's like . . . it's like my head is all wrapped up in cotton. It's like the color has bled out of my life and all that's left is black and white. I wanted to experience Cameryn without the meds." She leaned forward, her face flush with excitement as her voice rose, almost shrill. "Justin, since I stopped I've felt so much better. I'm on *fire* again. All those years of doing what the doctors told me. They were wrong. I stopped medicating myself and something woke up inside. I've got my energy and I feel like I'm *alive*!"

The knowledge twisted through Cameryn like a

snake. Her mother had stopped taking medication because of *her*.

"Is that why you came to see me?" Hannah asked. "To make sure I'm on my meds? As far as I know, failure to take medication is not a crime."

"That's not why, Hannah." Justin's voice was gentle. "I came because of our Baby Doe. We've got a name for her now. The victim was Esther Childs."

"Esther?" Hannah paused. She sat back in her chair, crossing her arms over her chest tight, as if to hold herself in.

"Have you ever seen this girl before? I'm talking about Saturday, December ninth. Here's what she looks like." Justin handed Hannah a picture.

Hannah glanced at the photograph and gave an exaggerated shrug. "No. I've never seen her."

Justin paused. "We have a witness who saw the two of you together. You and Esther. Our witness said you were talking to the girl in your blue Pinto shortly before she died."

Cameryn's heart beat wildly as she watched her mother's face go through a range of expressions. Cocking her head, Hannah pulled the photograph within an inch of her eyes.

"Who told you they saw me?" she asked.

"A man from town. Don't lie, Hannah. Just tell me what happened."

"I was confused because of the hair. The girl I picked up had long hair."

"So you recognize her now?"

"I think she might be the child I found at the gas station. But then she ran away and I never saw her again." Hannah returned the picture. "That girl's death has nothing to do with me."

"I'm sure it doesn't," replied Justin. "But I need to ask you some questions, and I want you to answer honestly. This has turned into a homicide investigation. The rules have changed."

"Homicide." Hannah's hands grabbed her elbows so hard Cameryn could see the jut of every knuckle. "Cameryn told me it was a suicide."

"That's what we thought at first. But we were wrong."

"So you were wrong." Hannah jumped to her feet. Still clutching her arms she began to pace the room. "Talking to a girl isn't a crime. All I did was talk to her. What are you saying, Justin? What are you implying?" Her voice had become high and frightened. "I thought you came as a friend and you've come as a deputy. You're here thinking—Why *are* you here?" She caught Cameryn's eye and shrieked, "Cammie!"

Cameryn felt her skin jump at the sound of her name. The door swung open. Justin stared at her, his eyes electric, but he didn't get up. In his hand he held a notebook and a pen.

"Cammie called me right before you came, Justin," Hannah insisted. "Right before you came. She says she knows who committed the murder."

"What do you know about this?" he asked her quietly.

Her mind worked furiously. Hannah didn't know that the clues had tied together through the ring. How could she? But the truth had to come out, so there was nothing to do now but tell it.

"Esther left this ring in my mother's car," Cameryn said, pulling it from her pocket. "Here, take it."

With thumb and forefinger, Justin lifted it from her open palm. He peered at it, then at her, stunned. "When did you get this?"

"Yesterday."

"So you knew—?" But Cameryn cut him off with, "Look at what it says. 'Keep Sweet.' I wrote Jo Ann Whittaker. She did some research—"

His eyes flashed. "You shared information about an active homicide case—"

"Justin, please, let me finish." Cameryn took a breath. Hannah had stopped moving and was staring. Everything had become suddenly still, as if the room itself were holding its breath. "Jo Ann found out that 'Keep Sweet' is a saying used by Fundamentalist polygamists. If Esther had that ring, she was from a polygamist family." Cameryn turned to her mother. "What did she say to you when she put it in the cup holder?"

"She said she didn't need it anymore."

"Right. She was running away. Girls her age are married off, and I bet she didn't want to be. Except they're not allowed to leave. Remember, Justin, how strange her underwear looked? We saw the polygamists on the street, how the women were dressed. . . . I think Esther was running, and she got caught. And her hair was cut off. I'll bet that's something they would do." Cameryn looked from Justin to her mother. "We need to check it out."

"Tell me this again," Justin said. "Slowly this time."

She did, filling in each detail as she repeated everything. There'd be trouble ahead for her, she realized that, but as her words tumbled over each other, it felt so good to free herself from the guilt she'd been carrying. Every part of the story came out, even about the wallet. "Esther must have been pretty desperate. I mean, I don't think she looked like a thief, but she was. Justin, when I thought it was a suicide I didn't see any reason to tell."

"So, Esther stole your mother's wallet."

"Yes."

"And you think she must have chucked it in a garbage can before the polygamists shot her."

"Or maybe they took it. I don't know. It wasn't at the autopsy."

"You mean this wallet?" Justin stood and walked to her mother's dresser. The oak top was covered with a lace doily, and there, on top, lay her mother's brown leather wallet. Cameryn had seen it before. It had a small gold tab with the words DOONEY & BOURKE stamped above the image of a goose.

Behind her, Cameryn heard her mother's voice cry, "Oh my God, Cammie. I promise, I can explain."

Cameryn, her muscles growing tight as wires, stared at the wallet as Justin picked it up.

"No, look at me, Cammie," Hannah begged, the skin on her face blanching to the same sickly color Mariah's had taken in death. "I can explain," Hannah cried wildly. "Cammie—all right—you've found my wallet and I know it looks bad. That's why I didn't tell before. I wanted to but I *couldn't*."

Too stunned to speak, Cameryn blocked her mother out. Justin undid the wallet's clasp and there was her mother's driver's license, the credit cards shining from their plastic sleeves. There was no mistake. It belonged to Hannah. All the other noise of the world seemed to have gone silent; the only sound was blood pulsing through her ears.

"Cammie, look at me." Her mother gripped Cameryn's arm, but Cameryn's eyes dropped to the floor. "Please, Cammie! Justin." Riveting her gaze on the deputy, she cried, "I know how it looks, but you have to understand. I kept searching for Mariah and I thought I saw a patch of blue, so I went down that alleyway. I swear to God when I saw her, Mariah—Esther—she was already dead. I swear to *God*." The eyes were back on Cameryn now; she could feel the intensity of her mother's stare. Hannah cried, "I swear on Jayne's grave and on anything else. You've *got* to believe me! I saw the backpack and I thought"—her grip became iron—"I thought—this girl is already dead. I didn't want anyone to know. So I took what was mine."

A blankness filled Cameryn, as if her mind couldn't absorb her mother's words. Nothing could penetrate.

"Are you listening?" The claw on Cameryn's arm clamped so hard she almost cried out in pain. "I want you to leave now, Deputy," Hannah raged. "I want you to leave my room."

"As much as I want to," Justin said, his voice low, "I can't."

Hannah stood rigid for a moment, and then, almost imperceptibly, began to rock back and forth. "I'm going to go to jail. You're going to take me to jail." The rocking increased in intensity: forward and back, backward and forward. "I didn't do it," Hannah cried. "I didn't. Cameryn, you're the only one. You've *got* to believe me!"

Justin stepped forward. He shoved his notebook in his back pocket, and then carefully, gently, peeled away Hannah's fingers from Cameryn's arm, as though they were petals from a closed flower. He looked as though he felt sick. His own fingers trembled as he took a step backward.

"I'm sorry, Cammie," Hannah whispered. "I'm sorry about everything."

"Hannah, I want you to listen to me carefully," Justin said. "Can you hear me? Do you understand what I'm saying?"

Dropping her hands to her sides, Hannah sobbed a single word: "Yes."

"I need to make sure you know what I'm saying."

"I do. I do, I do, I do."

"Then, Hannah . . ." He paused. His next words were delivered quietly but clearly. "You have the right to remain silent. . . ."

Chapter Fourteen

THE SILVERTON COUNTY jail was situated inside one of the town's most beautiful buildings. The county courthouse, a square-faced, steep-roofed affair, had a large circular clock mounted in the middle of a three-tiered steeple. The stone was gray, Protestant-looking. Cement pillars and roof protected the front door from the elements. An ecclesiastical window had been carved from the stone, giving the mayor a bird's-eye view of the town. But this morning, Cameryn didn't notice any of that. It was *who* the building contained that mattered to her. Hannah had been cuffed and taken away to the one-room jail, and even though Cameryn pleaded to stay with her mother, Justin refused.

"Cammie, you're not allowed to come with me," he'd said as Hannah stood rigidly to one side. Justin's face had flushed with agitation. "God knows I hate to do this, but I have to take her in."

Cameryn grabbed his sleeve, wrenching it in her hand. "You *can't!*"

"I have no choice. She had the decedent's property. She's got a motive and she's been off her meds."

"Justin, *no!*"

"There's an eyewitness who's placed Hannah with the vic just moments before she was shot. And now I know she was with Esther *after* she died."

"But there was an explanation. She told you why—"

Justin shook his head. "She's also a flight risk. If I don't take her in I could lose my job. Let me do this and then we'll sort it all out."

To that, Cameryn had cried, "Of *course* you have a *choice.*" But Justin didn't seem to hear.

Now, as she walked down the polished wooden hall-way, the heels of her boots reverberating in the empty hall, she rehearsed her strategy. Although she was angry with Justin, it was important not to let emotion show. Like it or not, she needed him. She took a breath and shook herself, trying to focus, trying to be strong. With her knuckle she rapped on the glass pane sten-cilcd with a golden star and the words SHERIFF'S OFFICE in black letters.

Justin opened the door, not all the way, just a few inches. He looked rumpled, tired. "Hey."

"Hey yourself."

"Our office doesn't officially open for twenty minutes."

"Len opened the courthouse early and I followed him inside," she said. "I told him I was meeting you. Were you here all night?"

"I had to be," he answered. "It's against the law to leave a prisoner unattended. I semi-slept in the chair."

"Can I come in?"

Justin sighed. "You can't see her, Cammie. She's in a holding cell. No visitors."

"That's okay." Cameryn wedged her foot between the door and the door frame. "I want to talk to you."

He studied her a moment. The stubble on his chin had grown, his hair was tousled, and his lids were hooded from lack of sleep. Reluctant, he opened the door and allowed her inside. "Shouldn't you be in school?"

"I'm taking a day off."

"Whoa, whoa, whoa," he croaked. "You're cutting school?"

"Yeah. I am."

"You *never* cut school."

"Right." Cameryn felt a pang of guilt. In all her years of education, she'd never once skipped school. But there was a first time for everything. Her mother needed her.

"You're already in trouble with the sheriff, Cammie. Guess you're going all the way. Have a seat." The room was so crowded with filing cabinets and plants and Sheriff Jacobs's big wooden desk, there was room only for two folding chairs for visitors. To the left, beside a painted radiator, was Justin's chair, half the size of Jacobs's. Everything for Justin seemed miniaturized—stacks of papers towered on a surface barely wide enough for his computer. He grabbed one of the folding chairs and placed it across from his desk, pointing for Cameryn to sit.

His own chair squeaked as he leaned forward. "So what's up?"

"You seem tense," she began.

"Well, you called me just about every name in the book last night. Maybe my 'tenseness'"—he made quotation marks with his fingers—"has something to do with that."

"Yeah, well, I'm sorry. I was just upset."

"Obviously." Justin picked up a pen and hit the black plastic cap onto a clear spot on his desk, flipped it, then hit the pen again. "How did your pop and your grandma handle the news?"

"They said I should wait and see where your investigation leads before I panic. My dad's really mad at me for withholding evidence. *Really* mad. But he said he understood why I did it. My mammaw went to church and said a rosary. She thinks I'm going to have a long stay in Purgatory if I don't get my act together."

Justin put down his pen and knit his fingers together. He leaned forward and spoke softly. "We're holding her for seventy-two hours and she's back on her meds, which is a very good thing. The district attorney will review the facts of the case. He'll make the decision on whether to file charges or not."

"Yeah, I know how it works."

"I *had* to take her in, Cammie. I wish you'd understand."

"I do," she lied. Today she'd worn her hair in a ponytail and had on a blue Fort Lewis sweatshirt, along with her heavy winter parka. Unzipping her coat, she slipped it off and asked, choosing the words carefully, "But there are other leads, aren't there? Like my theory about polygamy?"

He pulled back again. The wheels screeched against the tile. "What about it?"

"Are you going to research it or not?"

"There is nothing to research. The Childs family is from Arizona. Their hometown sheriff says they're not polygamists and the entire family was there the day Esther was killed. The sheriff personally saw them."

"But but " Camcryn stammered, "the ring . . ."

"Our vic could have picked it up anywhere."

She leaned forward, her eyes narrowing. "We *saw* polygamists."

"There are polygamists all over," Justin said, his voice rising.

"Well, what about the name Gilbert, the name I found written in the backpack? I looked it up on the Internet, and there's a Gilbert two doors down from the Loaf 'N Jug, where that phone tip came from. Don't you think that's strange? That's a lead."

"Which I checked out yesterday. The woman's name is Ruth Gilbert. She didn't make the phone call and she didn't know a thing about Esther. It's a dead end."

Cameryn tried to keep the panic from her voice. "But the backpack had the name *Gilbert* printed on it—"

"And Ruth said she gave a load to Goodwill. Esther could have picked it up there. It doesn't prove anything. Cameryn, I know how hard this is for you, but you've got to let us handle it from here. We're the law. You're the slice-and-dice."

Inside, there was a tremor, but like a magician perfecting the slight of hand she would not let him see it. "Can I take a look at the file?" she asked. "That one, right there." A manila folder lay open on his desk and she could see it had her mother's name on it. "I want to see it."

"Cammie, this is police business."

"*Please.* Justin, no one'll know."

Slowly, he turned the folder her way and pushed it toward her across his desk. She could feel him watch her as she scanned the pages, one after the other until she saw what she was looking for. Closing her eyes briefly, she committed the number to memory: 928–555–6823.

"Hannah is my friend, too," he told her as he pulled the folder back. Slowly, he closed it and set his hands on top, folded, as if in prayer. "I've called in Dr. Kearney and he's going to do an evaluation. I got her to take her meds. She made me a list of books she'd like and I'm going to the library to pick them up. We're doing the best we can."

"But you still arrested her," Cameryn stated, rising to her feet. Then, shrugging on her coat, she walked to the door, past the sheriff's gun rack and his filing cabinet and his belt full of bullets curled on top. Her hand was on the doorknob when she heard Justin call out, "I could have lost my job."

Cameryn turned to look at him, at his tousled hair and blue-green eyes and the way he was pleading with her to forgive him. "I get that, Justin. I really do. It's just—it's worse to lose a mother."

She was barely inside her car before she fished out a pen and wrote the phone number onto her palm in ink. 928–555–6823. The sun struggled to break over the mountains as she sat, shivering, in the frosted light. The parking lot was already beginning to fill up with county workers. In an effort to be discreet, she had parked beneath a stand of bare aspens, hoping the sheriff wouldn't recognize her car. Branches shifted in the winter breeze, creating an intricate, dancing pattern on the dashboard of her car. For a moment she watched the shadows, thinking.

There was no one to help her mother. Not the sheriff or Justin or her father or her mammaw—she, Cameryn, was the only one Hannah could count on. The wallet, the ring—it didn't mean anything. Her mother stayed locked away, yet innocent, as only Cameryn believed. But belief was not enough. It was action she needed.

One tenuous thread remained for her to follow, a silver strand of chance that might connect the Gilbert family to Esther. Maybe. If God was with her.

With her BlackBerry freshly recharged, she crossed herself. First, she entered *67 in order to block her number in case the Childs home had caller ID. Then she punched in the digits, holding her breath, waiting.

"Hello?" a gruff man's voice answered.

"This is Amy Green from the sheriff's office," Cameryn began, stealing the name of her father's friend in Ouray. Craning her neck to make sure she was still alone, she said, "I have a question concerning Esther Childs. First, let me begin by saying I'm really sorry for your loss. Are you the father?"

"I am. We're trying to cope the best we can. What's your question?"

Cameryn swallowed. "I'm currently researching a possible link between Esther and polygamy. Esther had a ring on her finger that had the words "'Keep Sweet.' We're trying to track that down."

It took a moment for the man to answer, so long Cameryn wondered if they'd lost the connection. "I don't know nothing about that," he finally said. "We're respectable people down here. If Esther had it, I don't know where she got it from."

"I'm investigating a possible source. There's a woman in Durango named Ruth Gilbert—"

It was then she heard an audible intake of air as he gasped.

Blinking, she asked, "Do you know her? Mr. Childs, do you *know* a Ruth Gilbert?"

"No," he said, and Cameryn could tell he was lying.

Pressing the BlackBerry closer to her ear, she said, "Perhaps Ruth Gilbert was the one who gave the ring to your daughter. Could that be possible?"

"How would I figure that? That's somethin' you'll have to investigate. I already told you I've never heard of the woman. Our child is dead and you're makin' her out to be in some kind of cult. What's your name again?"

"Um, the sheriff needs me right now. Good-bye, Mr. Childs, and thank you for your time. We'll get back to you when we have more information," she concluded the call at a gallop and tried to calm her racing thoughts. As the shadows played across her dashboard, she thought of the interconnection of the two lives and wondered what it could mean. Mr. Childs knew Ruth Gilbert. He could deny it all he wanted, but she'd heard it in his voice. What she had in mind would be crazy, could get her into even more trouble, maybe even fired from her job. She didn't care. Shifting her car into reverse, she headed out once again, for Durango.

It was time to find answers.

Chapter Fifteen

THE HOUSES ON the south side of Durango were different from the homes in Silverton. These were small places, rectangular and utilitarian, painted in softer tones than the Easter-egg colors splashed on the dwellings throughout Cameryn's town. Durango was more upscale and respectable. Trees lined the streets, their empty branches webbed with Christmas lights. It was eight A.M., and already the streets were humming with traffic. Countless people hurrying along the shoveled walkways of College Drive.

Heading east, she saw the Loaf 'N Jug, where the call had been made. Reflexively, she slowed her Jeep to a near stop, searching the building until she saw it: the pay phone, hanging on the front wall, protected by a three-sided metal box. At that moment it was being used by a man with long, straw-colored Rastafarian dreadlocks that splayed like octopus tentacles from beneath a multi-colored knit cap. As he talked he gestured wildly, his free hand jabbing the air, and Cameryn realized if there had been any latent prints they were long gone, rubbed into obscurity by countless hands.

Beep-beep!

In her rearview mirror she saw a man honking at her impatiently. Waving, she gunned her engine and drove, making a sharp right onto Sixth Street. Two doors down was the Gilbert home. She parked, trying to steady her breathing. If she did this right, she had a shot. But it would be just one.

Ahead of her was an elementary school, overrun with vans and cars disgorging children onto the front walkway. She looked at the crumpled address she'd tossed onto the passenger seat, next to her Map Quest directions that showed her the way in bright yellow ink.

"Well, this is it," she told herself softly. "Play it cool." She grabbed her notebook and jumped out of her car. Trying to look confident, she made her way up the walkway lined with two rows of candy canes, the kind that lighted up from the inside in bright red and white stripes. A large Santa had been taped to a window, and a yellow plastic sled was propped on the side of the house. With a shaking finger, she pressed the doorbell, listening to its distant chime, hoping she looked old enough to be the college student she was about to claim to be. Cameryn waited, then rang the bell again. Maybe the house was empty—most people worked during the day. Maybe her crazy drive down here had all been for nothing.

A woman with a baby slung on one hip answered the door. "If you're selling somethin' I'm afraid I don't want any," she said. The woman wore a pink sweat suit emblazoned with a teddy bear holding a flowered wreath. Her hair was blonde and thick, and her eyes were a pale blue—the same palette, Cameryn remembered, that had appeared on Mariah's perfect features. The door was just swinging shut when Cameryn cried, "No! Please! I'm a student up at the Fort, and I just need to ask you a few simple questions. It's for my class and so far no one will help me. I mean, nobody's home anymore. I've been knocking on doors all morning."

Since Fort Lewis College was only two miles away, claiming to be a student there should make a good cover. She held her breath as the door swung back open. "What class?" the woman asked, eyeing her suspiciously.

"Psychology. This is my first year. Please, it'll only take a few minutes. You'd really be helping me out a lot." When the woman hesitated, Cameryn turned her attention to the baby in the woman's arms. The child had the same champagne coloring as the mother, along with fat, cherubic cheeks. "Is that a boy or a girl?"

"Girl."

"She is so *cute*! What's her name?"

"Adriel."

"That's a pretty name! I've never heard it before. That's, like, the prettiest name ever. If I have a baby girl someday, I'll have to remember that name. Hi, little Adriel!" Cameryn could tell she was going over the top, pressing too hard, but she worried the door might slam shut any minute, so she filled space with a torrent of words. When she looked up, the woman was smiling.

"All right, all right—I'll bet part of your psychological experiment is seeing if you can get into a house by charmin' the baby." There was something familiar in her voice, something Cameryn couldn't quite place. "You're sayin' it's a *short* survey?"

"Ten questions, that's it."

"Well, if you don't mind that I'll have to feed Adriel here while we do it, come on in." The woman opened the door wider.

"Thanks so much! My name is Cameryn, by the way." Cameryn extended her hand.

"I'm Ruth." Ruth gave Cameryn's hand a quick shake. "Don't look at my house—it's an awful mess. That's what happens when you've got a lot of kids. Follow me."

Contrary to what she'd said, the house, although cluttered, was clean. Photographs of children marched up the wall like stair steps, and a piano, buried beneath a flurry of sheet music, had been topped with more family pictures in shiny silver frames.

"How many kids do you have?" Cameryn asked, stepping over a Tonka truck as she followed Ruth's retreating figure.

"Seven."

"Wow! *Seven* kids!"

"Yeah. I get that a lot. Have a seat at the table there. Sorry, just move that cereal bowl. The rest of 'em are in school—thank heavens for mornin' kindergarten. Can I get you anything?"

Cameryn slid into a vinyl-covered chair. "If it's no trouble, I'd love a cup of coffee."

"Sorry, I can't help you there. We're members of the Church of Jesus Christ of Latter Day Saints, so we don't drink coffee."

"Oh. I didn't know that—I mean that you don't . . ." Cameryn blushed, feeling as though she'd committed a faux pas. "Um, then, could I have some tea?"

Ruth smiled and pulled the tray off a sage-green high chair. With an expert motion she slid Adriel inside and snapped the tray back on. "We don't drink tea, either. Except herbal, and I don't have any. How about some juice?"

"Juice would be great. Or water. Anything's fine."

"Let me get this one settled, and I'll get it for you."

The kitchen opened directly to the family room, which

had been turned into a kind of playroom. A toy plastic kitchen lined one wall and there was an old rocking chair that looked as though it was a family heirloom, carved in an intricate pattern across the top. Cameryn noticed a large photograph, this one featuring what must be the whole Gilbert family in a studio portrait with an artificial backdrop that resembled green suede.

"Do you mind if I look?" Cameryn asked, gesturing toward the portrait.

"Go right ahead. Four girls, three boys, ages ten down to nine months. That's my husband Charlie, the one who's responsible," she said with a laugh.

"What does your husband do?"

"He works for a company called Lore International. He's out of the country right now—been gone all week." Ruth looked at her, her face hopeful. "Do you babysit?"

"Not very often," Cameryn said. "You know, because of school."

"I never can get anyone to do it. Here's your juice," she said, setting down a glass of apple juice on a place mat. "So what are your questions?"

Pulling herself away from the portrait, she slid into a chair and opened her notebook. Removing her pen, she clicked the end, trying to look official. "My report is on people's perception of the role of government. Would you identify your home as Democrat or Republican?"

"Republican. But just so you know, not all Mormons

are Republican. There are a lot in my ward that are Democrats, too."

"Ward?"

"That's what we call the buildings where we go to church."

Cameryn checked a box on the printed-out form she'd constructed just that morning. All night she'd tossed and turned, trying to come up with a plan to get the information she needed, until she'd hit on the idea of a survey. That was just one more breech of forensic protocol that could get her fired, but everything she'd done lately could cost her her job. Even cost her the scholarship. *Don't think about that now. Just do it. See where this goes.*

"So, Ruth, do you vote?"

"Every election." She shoved a small spoonful of baby food into Adriel's mouth; the baby promptly spit it back out. Scooping it up with the side of the plastic spoon, Ruth slid the food back into the open mouth, parting her own lips as she did so.

"Do you regularly attend church?"

"Yep. Every Sunday."

Cameryn marked another meaningless box. Her hands began to sweat as she asked, "Do you believe in the death penalty?"

"Yes," Ruth answered firmly. "A life for a life."

"Right." Cameryn checked her sheet. "Now, speaking of the death penalty, do you personally know anyone who has been murdered?" She said this quickly, without looking at Ruth's face. She could hear Ruth pause as she studied her paper.

"What class did you say this was for?"

"Psychology."

"What's the name of your teacher?"

"Ms. Dunham," Cameryn said, lying with the first name that popped into her head. "So do you know anyone who has been the victim of a murder?" she repeated.

Silence. When she spoke, Ruth's voice had grown dim. "No. Never."

"Have you—have you been following the case of Baby Doe in the *Durango Herald*?"

"No."

"They have a name for her now. It's Esther Childs. Someone made an anonymous call from the Loaf 'N Jug. That's right by your house, isn't it? The Loaf 'N Jug. It was called in to Silverton."

No answer.

"The woman tipped the police as to the victim's true identity." Cameryn slid a newspaper from the inside of her folder. The color had drained from Ruth's face, and Cameryn noticed she was trembling. It was as if they'd each had a stick that sparked against the other and the fire was taking hold, burning. "Look," Cameryn said, tapping her finger on the picture. "Do you see the girl? Have you ever seen her before?"

Esther's death had made front-page news. The sketch of the girl showed eyes wide and clear, the hair plaited in the long braid. Cameryn positioned the paper so that the face was dead center on the table.

The baby made a gurgling sound and smacked her hand impatiently on her tray.

"I have a lot to do. I think I'm done with your survey," Ruth said, standing up.

Desperate, Cameryn said, "Esther had on a ring that said 'Keep Sweet.' You know about 'Keep Sweet.' Don't you, Ruth?"

"You're not here for a psychology class."

"I'm not," Cameryn admitted. "I'm sorry, but there are things I'm trying to find out."

As Ruth pulled her baby out of the high chair, she took a step back so that she was against a wall. Pure fear radiated from her eyes. "Who are you, then? Are you a Messenger?"

It took a moment for her to register what Ruth was saying. "Am I a what?"

Ruth began pacing, chastising herself. Adriel was perched on her hip. With every step, the baby's head bounced like a doll on a spring. "How could I have been so stupid? They knew I wouldn't open the door for a man, so they sent you. I see your long hair. You're living the Principal. You're checking up, seeing if I talked. You go back and tell the Prophet it *wasn't me*!" Ruth clutched her baby so hard Adriel cried out. "You need to leave. Now! Tell him!"

"Tell who what?" Cameryn's mind was working and working and she couldn't think this through. "Ruth, I'm not a Messenger."

"I want you out of here!" she demanded. She pointed to her front door. "Now!"

"I'm sorry," Cameryn answered softly. "I can't."

She stayed planted in the wooden chair, the rungs pressing into her back. Looking at the blue plastic bowl and the dried cereal, she tried to make her mind put together the pieces. Something had frightened Ruth deeply, but fear wasn't anything Cameryn could take to the sheriff. What she needed was proof. If she waited, Ruth could pull herself together and deny the conversation even happened. Cameryn opened her folder and set out a photograph she'd printed from her camera. It was a close-up of Esther's face. The eyes stared, wide and blank.

"I work for the coroner's office," Cameryn said. She pulled another photograph of Esther and set it next to the first. This one showed the bullet hole in the side of her skull. "Somebody shot her. Shot Esther. In cold blood."

Ruth raised her hand to her mouth, and Cameryn heard an angry, muffled groan. Her face had gone scarlet. "Put those away," she cried. "I can't look at them!"

"You have to look," Cameryn told her, "because the authorities are trying to say my mother did this." Cameryn pulled another picture from her folder. The boot print in the center of Esther's back showed up in sharp relief. "Whoever did this cut off Esther's hair. Fourteen years old and her life was taken. I think you made that call from the pay phone because you know this girl. That's right, isn't it?"

Ruth nodded. "She was my niece," she said. Tears streamed down her face. "My sister's child."

Cameryn's heart raced wildly as she formed her next question. "Do you know who killed her?"

Her mouth moved, but her words were only a whisper. "I do."

Cameryn felt elation until she heard what came next: "I know exactly who killed her. But I will never, ever tell."

Chapter Sixteen

THEY SAT STARING at each other. Cameryn counted the seconds as they ticked away on the kitchen clock. They baby began to wiggle in Ruth's arms, but she held her tight. "Just so you understand," Ruth said, "I'll deny everything I just told you. I can't help you, Cameryn. I wish I could but I can't." She set the baby down on a brightly quilted blanket that had been tucked inside a playpen. Then she gathered up the photographs of Esther and shoved them into the folder. "I want you to leave my house."

"You know who killed this girl and you won't tell?" Cameryn cried.

"I know who killed this girl and I *can't* tell. Because they said they'd kill me. Me and my family." The voice edged on panic.

Cameryn rose to her feet. Her blood rocketed as she cried, "But they're accusing my mother!"

Ruth's fingernails dug so hard against the edge of the table they looked bloodless. "I converted to the Church of Jesus Christ of Latter Day Saints years ago. I have a good life now. That nightmare is over for me."

"And my mother's in a jail cell in Silverton! She's *in* a nightmare!" Cameryn practically screamed the words, her hands gesticulating wildly. Suddenly, Ruth grabbed Cameryn's left wrist in her hand. Her grip was like iron as she turned Cameryn's palm up. "What's that?" she shrilled, pointing to the digits written on her skin. "That's the Childses' number. Did you call them?" Her eyes narrowed. "Did you ask them about me?"

"Yes—I—"

"Did you mention me by name? *Did you mention me by name?*"

"I might have. I . . . I was trying to figure things out. I said I was with the sheriff's office and—"

"When! How long ago?" Ruth jerked Cameryn so hard her feet almost left the floor. She was solid, tall, and deceptively strong. Her nostrils flared as she cried, "When did you make that call?"

"An hour ago. Maybe an hour and a half . . ."

"You don't know what you've done!" Ruth released her and Cameryn staggered back. "I have to get out of here!" she cried, her face contorted, her expression frantic, wild.

"The drive is only three hours from Placement. I still have time."

"If you're worried, then call the police!" Cameryn told her.

"*No!*" Ruth's pale eyes flashed. "You have no idea who these people are." She rushed to the refrigerator, yanking out item after item—milk, cheese, fruit, a bag of salad, a jug of orange juice—and shoving them all helter-skelter into a garbage bag. "I can't do anything until my kids are safe."

"Safe. Safe from what?"

"They warned me once. I helped smuggle girls out of polygamy, and they warned me. When Esther came here, I sent her away. They found her and they killed her and cut off her braid. It's what they do, the way they take a girl's beauty, the way they leave their mark. So the blood is on my head. The circle of blood has come back to me."

Leaving the bag of food on the counter, Ruth grabbed two more garbage bags and raced upstairs. Cameryn followed, not knowing what else to do. "Leave," Ruth cried, turning on her. "*I want you out of my house!*"

"If you're scared, there are safe houses!"

Ruth laughed harshly. "You don't understand. These people find you no matter where you hide. Why do you think I sleep with a gun?"

"But—"

"Just *go!*" Ruth stormed into a room and Cameryn

trailed behind, arguing, begging, but Ruth refused to listen. The room was pink and white with a rosebud paper border, like a wedding cake. Stuffed animals were strewn everywhere. The beds, though, cheerful beneath matching quilts, had been neatly made. Helpless, she watched the woman rake through drawers and shove things into a plastic bag before rushing past Cameryn to the next room, this one painted blue. Once again, Ruth stuffed clothes and shoes into a bag until it bulged.

"I know of a place that's far away," Ruth huffed. "Far enough, I pray God, that they'll never find us." She hoisted the bags, one in each hand. Her body bent beneath the weight as she hurried down the hall toward the steps.

"But what about my *mom*!"

Ruth paused. "I'll do this: once we're safe, I'll call your sheriff in Silverton. We have to be safe first."

"How do I know you won't just disappear?" Cameryn demanded.

"You can't know," she answered. "That's just the thing, isn't it? You didn't know when you made that call that I'd have to go into hiding. You're trying to protect your mom, I'm trying to protect my kids, and we all go round and round. You opened a Pandora's box. These people are—"

Ruth didn't finish her thought because at that moment Adriel screamed a loud, high-pitched wail. Cameryn watched Ruth go white. "Oh, no . . ." The bags made a thud as she dropped them. "Stay here," she hissed. She stumbled down the stairs, taking them two at a time, rounding the corner out of sight. Cameryn's mind, which had been spinning frenetically, froze as she tried to comprehend.

"Put her down!" Ruth screamed.

Below, Cameryn heard a loud thud and a crunching sound, a muffled cry and a soft groan. Heavy footsteps preceded a man's voice, deep and low. It rumbled like a train through a tunnel. Cameryn shrank back against the wall as she heard him proclaim, "God's wrath is visited upon you and your children. You had your chance, Ruth Gilbert. You were warned. But you tossed aside our mercy. We've extended you charity time and again, and yet you spit in our face."

"No," Ruth cried, "I didn't—"

"You betrayed us," claimed a second voice. "Nephi told you our laws were not their laws. You've aided our women when they scorned the Principal. You, who have left the truth for a lie. You've brought the eye of the Gentiles to our community, and now they will descend upon us. What did you tell the sheriff in Silverton?"

"Nothing!"

"You *lie!*" Cameryn heard what sounded like skin hitting skin. "She said your name. What did you tell them?"

"I—I only told them who Esther was. So my sister could have her daughter. But nothing more! I swear!"

"*Liar!* You have brought this upon yourself."

Cameryn's heart pumped against her ribs. Quickly, quietly, she made her way down the hall to where she assumed the master bedroom would be. The guess was correct. A picture of a shining building hung over the large bed, with lights illuminating granite like strobes. The floor creaked beneath her feet as she punched 911 into her phone, and she prayed they wouldn't hear.

"This is 911. What is your emergency?" a female voice asked.

"I'm at 404 Sixth Street at the home of Ruth Gilbert," Cameryn whispered into her BlackBerry. "There's been a break-in. She's being attacked! Send help—*please*! I think the men are armed."

Cameryn heard a loud crunch and a scream.

"You say there are intruders—"

Ruth screamed again and Cameryn felt her blood run cold. "Hurry," she pleaded. "I have to go." As the operator began to argue, Cameryn hung up her phone and turned it off. Up here, she was hidden and safe. But she knew it took on average five minutes for the police to come to a crime scene. Horrible things could happen in that amount of time. She heard a slap against skin and the wail of the baby's cry.

The rough voice rang out again, "I got a call on my cell from the sheriff's office askin' about a Ruth Gilbert. That means you talked. Lucky for us we was already on our way here to pick up Esther's body." A riddled mass of nerves ran tight beneath Cameryn's skin. *She'd* made this happen to Ruth!

"It wasn't me!" Ruth wailed. Her voice sounded thick. The denial was followed by another horrible thud.

"Who, then!" the voice demanded.

"No, Nephi—!"

Another thump. "Who?"

"I don't know!"

A bang, this one like a blow from a hammer. "Give me a name if it wasn't you."

A choking sound, and then, "No one."

"Liar. You was packin' to leave. Do you think we're stupid? Is that what you think? Your soul will be consigned to outer darkness. You are an agent of Satan." This voice belonged to the second man. It was higher, thin and cold.

Cameryn heard whimpering and another horrible crash.

She almost jumped out of her skin when the phone rang, over and over, and she thought, *The police.* What if the dispatcher was calling back to make sure the case was real? What if, when there was no answer, they decided it was a hoax?

They were beating Ruth to death while Cameryn stood like stone. There was no time to wait. She would have to act.

"I'm begging you," Ruth gasped.

"You Jezebel! You harlot!" Nephi raged. A sound of flesh on skin, another pain-filled cry as Ruth began to weep.

"My—children!"

"Are as filthy rags. You have left the life of truth. Now you will surely pay."

No time left. Cameryn knew she had to move. *"Why do you think I sleep with a gun?"* Ruth had asked. Running her hands beneath the covers, she found nothing there. The floor squeaked again beneath her feet as she turned toward the nightstand. Ruth had left a reading lamp on, and in that light she gently, quietly, pulled open the drawer. Inside was a blue box marked COV-BAR .357 MAG-NUM AMMO. And behind it was—the gun. When she raised it up, it felt as big as her arm, long and unwieldy. She laid it on the bed and then pulled out the box of bullets. Her hands were shaking so hard it was almost impossible to open it.

More pounding and a scream from below. Cameryn, yanking at the cardboard lid, felt the box fly out from her fingers. Bullets rolled everywhere, like pennies from a broken roll, bouncing hard on the wooden floor. Swearing at herself, she squatted, opened the gun's chamber, and loaded a single pointed copper bullet into a cylinder. She could tell they had stopped talking. One of them asked, "Is someone else here? Seth—you check the upstairs."

Out of time! One bullet was all she'd loaded, but there

was no time left. Staggering to her feet, she ran down the hall, not caring if they could hear her footsteps as she pounded down the stairs. "*Stop!*" she screamed as she rounded the corner.

One man held Ruth by the hair, her blonde locks coiled around his wrist like a rope. Ruth's face was covered in blood and a pool of it stained the kitchen tabletop, a deep red blot the size of a dinner plate. Her eyes were so wide Cameryn could see the white all around, but it was the man she had to keep locked in her gaze. His hand clutched a gun, not yet fully raised. He stared at Cameryn, his face grizzled, his lip curled.

"I said stop!" she cried. "Drop your gun!"

"You're just a girl," the man said with disdain. He unwound his hand from Ruth's hair and gave her a shove. "You see that, Seth? Another Jezebel in this house of defilement." Nephi wasn't tall, but he looked strong, his arms thick with muscle. His buzzed gray hair topped a sunburnt face, seamed as elephant hide. A plaid cowboy shirt, the kind with piping and buttons that looked like pearls, gapped over his ample belly.

"I see her." Seth's blue cap with a stiff bill cast a shadow across his own weathered features. Both men wore boots, cowboy boots that came to a sharp point.

"Drop your gun!" Cameryn demanded again, her own gun so heavy she had to hold it with both hands. It shook in her grip.

"You know, Seth, I don't think she's got it in her," said Nephi, his voice suddenly cool. "Look at her shakin' like a baby." His own gun had begun to inch up, millimeter by millimeter. He was staring at her. Cameryn knew he was calculating his odds.

Her voice unnaturally high, she cried, "I know how to shoot."

"Do it, then. You're just a female. You think you're gonna shoot me? Then shoot me. But you've never killed, have you?" He grinned. "It takes a man to do that sort of thing."

Cameryn could barely breathe. She watched as Nephi's gun moved higher still. He was calling her out, his small eyes hard, challenging her.

She cocked the hammer and told him, "I'm warning you—"

"And I'm warnin' you right back," Nephi said. "You drop that gun, little girl. Drop it, and we'll go. No one will get hurt."

"Don't believe him!" Ruth cried.

Suddenly Nephi's arm jerked up and in the same second Cameryn squeezed the trigger of her Magnum. As the deafening blast burst through the air like a sonic boom, she felt a recoil so sharp she almost lost her footing. A blue lamp, inches away from Seth's head, exploded into thousands of tiny pieces, leaving bits of ceramic scattered across the carpet like mosaic tiles. Adriel let out a loud shriek and both Seth and Nephi jumped. She could sense shock and fury burning behind their immobile faces.

She'd used her one and only bullet. *But they don't know that,* she told herself. *Hold it together or we die.*

The men stared at her, wide-eyed.

"Put your gun on the floor and kick it to me," she commanded. "I'm serious. Kick it to me or I'll blow your freakin' heads off."

It was surreal. Cameryn, who didn't even like violent movies, was talking like she was in an old Clint Eastwood film. Neither one of them moved, so she said, "I'm not a girl, I'm a woman. And this is a Magnum. Do you really want to mess with a Magnum?"

Nephi's gun clattered to the linoleum. It was Seth who kicked it to her, the revolver spinning like a whirligig until it was stopped by a table leg.

"Ruth," Cameryn cried, "are you okay?"

Ruth nodded. Blood oozed out her nose, but she wiped it away. Her lip was cut and one eye had begun to swell. Leaning over, she picked up the gun. Ruth wobbled as she stood, but when she raised her arm, her aim seemed deadly. In a steady arc, the barrel moved from Nephi to Seth. Adriel sat crying in her playpen as Ruth said, "Hush, baby. It's okay now. Mommy's okay." When Ruth spoke, Cameryn saw that her teeth were coated in red. "Cameryn, can you call the police?"

A siren wailed in the distance. "I already did. That's them now."

Ruth croaked a single word. "Good." She swayed for a moment before righting herself. Keeping the gun pointed at the men, she walked past Cameryn to the front door, and throwing it open, she let in the light.

Chapter Seventeen

". . . AND SO YOU'RE saying that's when you shot the lamp," the corporal continued as he jotted down her words. "I'm sure those two have never seen spunk like that from a girl. You must have been quite a surprise."

"It was more of an accident than anything else," Cameryn said. "I've never shot a gun that powerful before. The kickback about knocked my arm out of its socket."

"It was enough to stop them."

She sat in a small interview room in the Durango Police Station, an older building cattycorner to the La Plata County Courthouse. Corporal Dunlop wore a regulation deep navy blue uniform, and he had a regulation haircut, too, buzzed flat on the top of his head. In the sparsely furnished room—just a metal table and two chairs—a small wall-mounted camera recorded everything she said, both audibly and visually. What the corporal wrote down, he told her, would be for his own files.

"Well, after two hours, I think I can safely say we're just about done," he announced, leaning back and stretching. "I'm sure you'd like to get out of here. Plus, I've got a truckload of people coming. The FBI is getting involved, and Social Services. That town over there in Four Corners was run lock, stock, and barrel by this Childs group. When your deputy . . . What's his name?"

"Crowley. Deputy Justin Crowley."

"Oh, yeah. When Crowley talked to the sheriff in Placement, he had no idea that the man he spoke with was actually their Prophet. Crowley obviously didn't get a straight story from the guy."

Cameryn twisted her hair around her finger like a ring. "I just don't get it—how could the rest of the state not know?"

"Don't be too hard on Arizona," the corporal told her. "That group lived in a closed community, way out on hardscrabble land. Their children were born without doctors. No birth certificates, no death certificates. Makes them hard to track. According to Ruth Gilbert, dissenters were executed and buried in the Childses private cemetery. The FBI will be in Placement tomorrow, searching for graves. And you," he said, smiling from behind his desk, "were the one who put it all together.

Why don't you forget about forensics? We lawmen could use someone like you."

He stood, signaling they were done. Cameryn, relieved, shook his hand and went down the stairs into the December sunshine. She was shocked to see Lyric and her boyfriend Adam leaning against her Jeep. Lyric laughed out loud as Cameryn halted, openmouthed.

"Surprise!" Lyric cried, running forward to hug her. "Justin called and told me what happened. Your dad's in Grand Junction—"

"Yeah." Cameryn hugged her friend back, hard. "Dad told me he's already turned his car around and is on his way home. I think I may be in for it."

"Well, I know someone who isn't mad. After all you've been through, *Justin* didn't want you to drive home alone. So *Justin* sent me. And Adam."

Grinning, Adam waved.

Lyric went on, "Justin called your dad who called the principal and *we* got a note. *We* are excused absences," said Lyric. "That boy has got it for you good, even when you treat him bad."

Lyric wore a lime-green parka with fuchsia trim, and a pair of striped knit gloves in green and yellow. A long-tailed ski hat with bells, bright pink, hung down her back. Locking arms with Cameryn, she said, "We're taking you to one of Adam's favorite spots. Stoners."

Adam finally spoke. "I think you'll like it," he said.

Always dressed in some version of black, today he wore black jeans and a long-sleeved T-shirt, no doubt sporting a skull or a headstone obscured by his dark, ankle-length coat. His hair, parted in the middle, hung in dark sheets, but his eyes were surprisingly warm. "It's close, right off of Main. It's got a good vibe."

"I could use a dose of that," Cameryn said. "Mammaw'll have to say a whole string of rosaries to keep me out of the flames."

Lyric squeezed her close. "I don't think they're mad, Cammie. Just worried. But you've had enough tension for one day. You solved the case, your mom's out of jail, so let's celebrate!"

Stoners turned out to be an organic café. Customers grabbed their own personal mugs off a peg board before ordering chai or oolong tea. Overhead, tie-dyed batiks billowed from the walls. Cameryn picked a mug with a picture of Einstein sticking out his tongue. A worn couch had been set next to a coffee table displaying an assortment of eclectic literature on the afterlife, the Buddha, the truth about Roswell's aliens, and vegan cooking. There was nothing in here she would possibly want to eat, Cameryn knew, but she didn't care. As they waited to be seated, Lyric and Adam peppered her with questions about polygamy and Seth and Nephi, talking above each other as Cameryn answered all she could. A sudden warmth infused her. Lyric, with her kohl-rimmed eyes, and Adam, his skin Edward Scissorhands–white, had driven all the way to Durango to help her. Cameryn, who'd found a girl's killer and freed her own mother from suspicion, could now relax in the company of her friends.

On the way back to Silverton—Lyric and Cameryn in the Jeep while Adam drove alone in his truck—Lyric admitted there was one more subject she'd been dying to talk about. "But not with Adam around," she said. "I wanted to wait for some privacy, so here's the thing. You and I—we've been friends forever, right?"

"Since grade school," Cameryn agreed, downshifting as the hill rose steeper.

"And friends tell friends the truth."

"Not if the friend of this friend has already had a really hard day."

"Come on, let me say it. I think it's really important." Lyric tucked a strand of purple hair behind her ear. Just last week Cameryn's grandmother had worried that Lyric's ever-changing hair color was too intense. "God made a person's hair the color that He wanted it to be, so it should be left at that," she'd said.

"Tell that to your friend Margaret," Cameryn had shot back. "It wasn't God who turned *her* hair blue."

"That was just a wee bit of a tint gone wrong. It's not the same thing at all," Mammaw had sniffed, but she'd said no more.

Now Cameryn sighed. She reset her mind in order to receive whatever it was Lyric was about to say. In her rearview mirror she saw the slash of Adam's face as his truck chugged behind them. "What is it? Are you having a psychic moment? Is my aura out of whack?"

"As a matter of fact," Lyric answered primly, "it is."

"*How* is it out of whack?"

"You're not seeing something that's clearly in front of you."

"Which is?"

"Justin."

Cameryn's hands tightened on the wheel.

"Justin really cares about you," Lyric said, twisting in her seat. She'd pulled off her hat, and her hair, full of static, crackled toward the roof of Cameryn's Jeep. "And stop rolling your eyes when I say his name. When Justin called me, he was panicked. Totally panicked. I thought he was going to have a meltdown because he couldn't drive down and be with you."

Instead of a negative feeling, a smile spread through Cameryn. "Really?"

"Really."

Cameryn's smile grew. Riding the day's victory made anything seem possible, maybe even stepping out of her reserve. Opening up. With Hannah set free and taking her medication, who knew what lay in store?

"That's a wicked grin, Cammie," said Lyric. "Seriously wicked."

It was a grin Cameryn wore all the way home.

* * *

Although it was only three o'clock in the afternoon, the lights from their Christmas tree were already on. Through the window Cameryn watched them blink on and off, casting small orbs of colored light against the living-room wall. She stood on the front stoop as if treading water, half afraid to go inside, but aware that she had no choice. Bracing herself, she opened the door, and almost immediately found herself in the arms of her mammaw.

"Good grief, child, what were you *thinking*? Going down to Durango like you were a spy." Mammaw hugged her tight, her hands like knots against Cameryn's back. Her grandmother smelled of cinnamon and cloves. "You could have been *killed*. And you cut school. You cut school and took off. That'll land you in trouble."

"I'm sorry, I was just trying to help."

"Your father'll be here any minute. Oh, don't look so worried, girl. We're both so relieved you're all right that nothing else matters. Have you seen Hannah?"

"I tried to call but she hasn't picked up. I thought maybe later I could go over to the Wingate and check on her."

"Let's see what your father has to say."

Cameryn heard the tires crunch in their driveway, followed by the bang of the kitchen door. She could feel the coolness of the Silverton air waft through the room, although that wasn't what made her shiver with goose bumps.

She saw him then, filling the doorway, but he didn't pause. Engulfing her in a bear hug, he yanked her to her feet and up into his arms, so that her toes barely touched the floor. As he kissed the side of her head roughly, he said, "Cammie, Cammie, Cammie, thank God you're safe."

"I'm okay, Dad," she murmured into his sweater. She could smell wet wool and the faint scent of his new after-shave, could hear the beating of his heart and feel the coarseness of his chin against her forehead.

"You're my only child," he told her, swaying her in his arms. "What would I do if something happened to you? What would I do then?"

Quietly, she answered, "I caught the killers."

He pulled away and stared. "You could have been shot. Come here. Sit down."

With his arm still around her, Patrick sank into the sofa, pulling her next to him. "I heard from Jacobs. He told me there's a graveyard for Fundamentalist girls who try to run. So far, they've found three others buried in the sand. Esther would have been the fourth."

Cameryn thought about this. She could hear a Christmas carol playing in the kitchen, soft and sweet. It was almost impossible to picture a life so different from her own. And yet, somewhere in Arizona there was a graveyard with young girls who had attempted to leave a life of forced marriage. Young, blonde slaves from the twenty-first century. She felt herself shiver again. "Why were they so angry with Ruth?"

"Because for a while she opened her home to the runaways. It was a safe house. That is, until Seth and Nephi found out and threatened her family. This time, when Esther showed up, Ruth gave her new clothes and a backpack, but she wouldn't let her stay."

"Oh, the poor woman," said Mammaw. "That's a lot of guilt she'll be feeling."

"If she hid the truth before, she's not hiding it now. She's in the hospital, recovering from a broken nose and shattered cheek. Remind me to send her flowers first thing in the morning." Touching Cameryn's cheek with his finger, her father said, "You should never have done what you did, and I could ground you forever—but you saved lives today."

"Hannah's life," Cameryn added quietly. "I think I saved her life, too."

"You very well could have. The case against her was circumstantial, but people have gone to prison on circumstantial evidence before." He laced his fingers through hers. "Cammie, you ultimately got to the truth. But . . . because of your mother, you withheld evidence in a murder case. Last summer you sat in that kitchen and begged me to hire you as assistant to the coroner. Your grandmother hated the idea."

"She still does."

"I'm beginning to accept it," her mammaw interjected. *"Beginning,"* she added when Cameryn shot her a look. Mammaw had dropped into the easy chair and picked up a large cloth Madame Alexander doll that needed a leg. With a hooked needle, she began to reattach a new limb, her hand moving as fluidly, Cameryn thought, as a surgeon's.

"When I put you on the payroll, you agreed to work for me. Not just father and daughter," he reminded her, "but employee and boss. Remember?"

She nodded.

"I want to talk to you now as your boss. You knew things about Esther's death that could have been crucial, yet you withheld the facts. Cammie, that's obstruction of justice. That's a very, *very* serious mistake."

"But it didn't matter—it doesn't matter. I was right, wasn't I? Hannah didn't do it. She didn't have *anything* to do with Esther's death."

Her father rubbed his hand over his eyes. "That's not the point. As a coroner, as medical examiners, our job is to reveal the facts. Reveal, Cammie, not conceal. There could have been legal ramifications for what you did."

"You mean legal ramifications for finding the truth?"

"You are not listening. If you were anyone else, you'd be fired. Do you understand?" He shook his head as she pleaded justification. "There is none," he said. "But we'll put this behind us and move forward. Because now I want to talk about your mother."

She knew where this was going, what he was about to say, but he surprised her. In a tender voice, he began, "Your mammaw and I talked, and we—I—Cammie, neither one of us has been fair to you. Or to Hannah."

She looked at him, disbelieving. Mammaw nodded her head while keeping her eyes on her needle and murmuring agreement. Ever since Hannah had reentered her life, Cameryn had felt as though they'd been locked in battle. Her grandmother's cantankerousness had equaled her father's firmness, and she, Cameryn, had matched both in her own quiet, stubborn way. But now the rules seemed to be changing. They were lining up together again, on the same side, the same team.

Patrick's heavy brows came together, creating a pleat between his eyes. "When your mother got . . . sick . . . I couldn't take it. But you've stuck by her. I'm proud of you for that."

"You have Amy Green now," she told him. "And you have Mammaw. Hannah's got no one but me."

"That was a mistake. My mistake. Our mistake. So I called her." His face contorted and his voice wavered as he said, "It's the first time I've talked to Hannah in almost fourteen years."

"It was the right thing to do," agreed Mammaw. "I see it now. It will be hard for us, but your father and I will try. We're going to try to make room for us all."

Cameryn sat, too stunned to speak. The flames of the fireplace danced as she tried to comprehend.

"I asked her to come to the house and she said yes," Patrick continued.

"Hannah? Here? When?"

"Any minute now. In fact, I think she's here."

Through the window Cameryn saw a figure make its way up the steps, heard the timid rap on the door. Leaping to her feet, she opened the door to see Hannah's pale face.

"Is this okay?" Hannah asked, her voice cautious.

Cameryn's eyes filled with tears as she threw the door wider. Light from the house brightened her mother's curly hair. In Hannah's outstretched hand she held a painting of an iris. "A gift," she said, "for your house."

And Cameryn, her throat so tight she could barely get out the words, answered, "Welcome to our home."

Chapter Eighteen

Cameryn was happy. It had been a long time since she'd felt so content, so full up with every good emotion. Her mother had come to their home, and her father had stood up to greet her. Awkwardly, he'd thrust his hands in his pockets when she'd walked in. Rocking on his heels, he'd examined Hannah while Mammaw, smiling stiffly, had offered her their most comfortable chair.

Hannah hadn't stayed long. Just a brush, a contact point, and then she was gone. But after she left, Mammaw had looked at the painted iris a long time before she put it on top of the piano. "I'll hang it in the morning," she'd said. "Not tonight."

And all the while Cameryn had beamed.

Now, stretching out on her bed, stomach down, she pulled her stuffed dog against her chest. There was no way to stop the memories that washed over her like an ocean at high tide. Her father, teaching her to fish, the line like a spider's thread in the waters of the Animas; her mammaw sewing an old doll's cloth arm while telling of her own Irish childhood in a brogue soft as a lullaby; the three of them huddled on the hard wooden pews of St. Patrick's, where her father nodded off while Cameryn laughed and her grandmother poked a sharp elbow into his side. This was her family, her past and present.

The future would soon add another thread. Her father had promised her that. Patrick, Hannah, Justin, her friends—they would weave their lives together into a new tapestry. It wouldn't be like it was before, but every thread would be strong. A beautiful cloth.

The soft ding of her computer brought her out of her thoughts. Someone had e-mailed her. Curious, she went to her desk and sat down, moving her mouse so that she could read her screen.

It was from Jo Ann Whittaker.

Dear Cameryn,

I was pleased to hear that you had a part in solving yet another difficult forensic case. This is precisely why we at Colorado University are so interested in your application. I hate to nudge, but I'm at home and I was hoping to ask you a few questions

concerning the original case that brought you to our
attention. As I write this, it is almost nine o'clock—a
bit late, I realize. But if you're at your computer and
available, I would like to clarify a few points. You
are part of a presentation that I will give tomorrow.

Typing quickly, Cameryn wrote:

> *Hi Jo Ann,*
> *I am here, at my computer. Ask me anything you'd*
> *like. I'm sorry I didn't fill out the form you sent, but*
> *I was very busy with the Jane Doe/Esther Childs*
> *case. I'll wait here for your next e-mail.*
> *Cameryn*

A minute went by before she heard another ding.

> *I am reviewing the case of Brad Oakes (the victim*
> *of Kyle O'Neil). It is an interesting study. I would like*
> *to ask you some specifics concerning your experi-*
> *ence. The decedent, Brad Oakes, was microwaved*
> *in his bed by a klystron tube. How did the body*
> *present?*
> *Jo Ann*

The good feeling she'd experienced evaporated as she
read the e-mail. Her teacher, Brad Oakes, had taught her

to love poetry. It was still hard for her to think about his death, the way he'd looked. She remembered it too well—his eyes blown out of his skull, and his withered body, arms pulled up, still clutching his bedsheet. The memory made her recoil, made her heart beat faster. Maybe Justin was right. Maybe she did need counseling.

Since she couldn't write that to Jo Ann Whittaker, she typed instead:

> *The body presented as though it had been burned, but burned from the inside out instead of the outside in. The internal organs near the head were cooked, while the organs lower down were not. I hope this is helpful.*
> *Cameryn*

She had already put on her pajamas when she heard another ding from her computer.

> *Thank you for your timely response. Because I am presenting to my colleagues, I would like a more complete answer to that last question. In other words, what did the body feel like? When you put your hands inside the cadaver, what was the sensation? Did your hands press against his ribs? At what point were you aware that his heart had been cooked? I understand the eyes actually blew out*

from their orbs. Is that correct? And for reference, can you tell me what your connection to your teacher was? How did your emotions affect your ability to perform an autopsy?

  Jo Ann

Cameryn sat, staring at the blinking curser. She was beginning to feel uncomfortable with the e-mail's tone. Part of her wanted to answer and part of her felt repelled by its strange nature. She chewed her lip. A moment later, she wrote: *I know this is for a presentation, but it is personally very difficult for me to deal with these issues. Would it be all right for me to pass on the last questions?*

Jo Ann's message chimed in only minutes later. It read: *No! I am counting on your complete honesty. Please respond to my specific questions.*

Cameryn squinted at the screen. The last e-mail made no sense. Why would her personal reflection be needed for a presentation? And yet, she knew it wouldn't be wise to offend the dean of forensics. She was about to type her answer, but she hesitated. Something was wrong—she could feel it. Instead of responding, she pulled out her BlackBerry and speed-dialed Dr. Moore.

"Hello," a grumpy voice began.

"Hi, Dr. Moore, it's me, Cameryn."

"Cameryn Mahoney. I hear through the grapevine that you solved our case. But it's almost nine o'clock. The wife and I have an early bedtime and I prefer to do business during office hours."

"I realize that. But I'm online, and I—I've been receiving e-mails from Jo Ann Whittaker."

"Lucky you," he said. There was a pause. "So what's the problem?"

In quick succession she recited the content of the e-mails she'd received. The phone line went silent, and for a moment she thought the connection had been lost. Finally Dr. Moore said, "Don't answer that last query. Wait. Let me get Jo Ann on my other line to see what she has to say. Hold on, Miss Mahoney."

"But—" she began.

"Just wait . . . I'll be right back."

Outside, wind raked the pines. The sound reminded Cameryn of water, of waves. She could hear Dr. Moore's deep rumble as he spoke on his other line. She couldn't make out his words, but the voice rose and fell and she almost got lost in the cadence of his rhythm. Suddenly she stiffened as she heard the word "fraud." A moment later, Dr. Moore was back on the line.

"Miss Mahoney, are you there?"

"Yes."

"I don't know what game this person's playing. . . ." He took a breath and said, "But Cameryn, I've been speaking with Jo Ann. She's never heard of you."

"*What?*"

"Listen to what I am saying!" His voice ratcheted up. "Whoever's been e-mailing you is *not* Jo Ann!"

It took a moment for the words to sink in. Cameryn sat, stunned. The cursor on her e-mail still blinked. For a moment she couldn't react.

"Cameryn!" Dr. Moore barked. "Are you there?"

The way he said her name made her jump. "Yes!"

"Turn off your e-mail. Shut down your computer. Do not respond to this crank."

"But my scholarship . . ."

Dr. Moore became impatient. "There *is* no scholarship. You've got some loony-tunes e-mailing you. I want you to hang up now and call the sheriff!"

In shock, still sitting at her desk, she heard another ping. On the subject line she read, *I C U.*

Her finger hesitated, but she opened it. She read: *Why aren't you answering? You should be answering. Because I see you.*

She was suddenly aware that her light was on in her room, of how it lit her up like a television screen. Through the gauzy sheer of her curtains she saw moonlight bright enough to frost the driveway, creating shadows. Their yard looked empty.

Seconds passed before she heard another e-mail chime.

I see you. Come out and play. Move your curtain and look out. By the trees. I'm waiting.

With a shaking hand, Cameryn turned off her light and pushed back the curtain. She peered outside, her pulse quickening as she searched the ground beneath her window. The moon was bright, casting shadows, throwing the trees into sharp relief. Wind had smoothed a shimmering crust of snow, softening the mounds until they looked like a turtle's back.

A shadow moved and she realized someone was out there. A figure stood half-hidden behind the arms of an evergreen.

Ping. She looked back at her screen. *I C U I C U I C U.*

Her eyes flew to the window. Beneath her, the shape of a male, tall, well muscled, with hair pale in the moonlight, had stepped from the shadow. Staring down, she saw the one face she never wanted to see again.

In the drifting snow stood Kyle O'Neil.

Acknowledgments

I'd like to thank the many people who helped me explore the forensic field. You have unselfishly shared your knowledge and passion-the glimpse into your world rocked mine! I'm especially grateful to: Thomas M. Canfield, MD, Fellow at the American Academy of Forensic Sciences, Chief Medical Examiner, Office of Medical Investigations; Kristina Maxfield, Coroner; Robert C. Bux, MD, Coroner, Medical Examiner, Forensic Pathologist; David L. Bowerman, Coroner, Forensic Pathologist, Dawn Miller, Deputy Coroner; Werner Jenkins, Chief Forensic Toxicologist; Chris Clarke, Forensic Toxicologist; Sandy Way, Administrator, El Paso County Coroner's Office; Sheriff Sue Kurtz, San Juan County Sheriff's Office; Melody Skinner, Administrative Assistant, San Juan County Sheriff's Office; Thomas Carr, Archaeologist, Colorado Historical Society; Richard Nanney, Douglas County Coroner Investigator; Sandy Graeff, Elbert County Coroner; Robert Brown, Agent-in-Charge, Colorado Bureau of Investigations; Jackie Kerwin, Silverton Librarian; Deb Cummins; Corporal Jacob Dunlop, Durango Police Department; and a special thanks to Robert Scott Mackey, D-ABMDI Deputy Coroner—an inspiriting professional and my conduit into a macabre world.

Alane Ferguson is the author of the Edgar Award Nominee *The Christopher Killer* and *The Angel of Death*—the first two books about Cameryn Mahoney—as well as numerous novels and mysteries, including the Edgar Award-winning *Show Me the Evidence*. She does intensive research for her books, attending autopsies and interviewing forensic pathologists as she delves into the fascinating world of medical examiners.

Ms. Ferguson lives with her husband, Ron, near the foothills of the Colorado Rockies. For more information about Ms. Ferguson and her books, please visit www.alaneferguson.com.